TIME FOR

JUL 07

CH

TIME FOR *Hope*

MAXINE BILLINGS

NEWSPIRIT

TIME FOR HOPE

A New Spirit Novel

ISBN-13: 978-0-373-83032-9
ISBN-10:   0-373-83032-7

© 2007 by Maxine Billings

www.kimanipress.com

Printed in U.S.A.

This book is dedicated to my dear friend JoAnn Turner.
Thank you for sticking with me through thick and thin.

… and there is a friend that
sticketh closer than a brother.

—*Proverbs* 18:24

ACKNOWLEDGMENT

To my Heavenly Father Jehovah, I thank you for blessing my writing efforts and for allowing me to continue giving my readers wholesome stories for their reading entertainment.

To my husband, Tony, daughter, Natasha, son, Stefan, and my *entire* family, thank you for your ongoing love, support, encouragement and patience. Without you, I could not go on.

To my agent, Pamela Harty, thank you for graciously extending yourself to me. It's nice to know that you're only a phone call or an e-mail away when I need you.

To my editor, Glenda Howard, I really appreciate all the hard work that you put into editing my manuscripts. Thank you for the encouragement and input that you share with me and for allowing me to continue to write for Kimani Press.

I would like to extend a special thank-you to:

The Harlequin and Kimani Press staff

Jamil and Shunda Leigh (Booking Matters)

Anna Royal, George Chip and Alexander High School of Douglasville, Georgia

Gwen Church and Hiram High School of Hiram, Georgia

Joe Livingston and Rick Couch (Neighbor Newspapers)

Rossie Colter, Philip Simmons and the Philip Simmons Foundation of Charleston, South Carolina

Prominent Women of Color Book Club of St. Marys, Georgia

Janet Payne and the Douglas County Connection
(a satellite of the Douglas County Cultural Arts Council)
of Douglasville, Georgia

And last but not least, to you—readers, the ones
who inspire me to write—thank you so much for your
warm expressions of support and encouragement.

Chapter 1

Spring in Chattanooga, Tennessee, was just about as pretty as autumn. Tyla Jefferson stood sipping her warm orange-spice tea, leaning against the wooden rails of the deck. The morning breeze was cool and gentle as it swept over her chestnut-colored complexion. She could see the tops of the pine trees and the bunches of golden-yellow daffodils that dotted the landscape. Tyla relished one last gaze before heading back through the French doors that led to the kitchen.

It was almost seven-fifteen. The excitement of starting her new part-time job today at Mercy Medical Center had gotten Tyla up at the crack of dawn. She had cooked breakfast for herself and her mother. She'd tried to wait for her mother to get up before devouring her own food; however, by seven o'clock she'd lost her restraint and packed away a good amount of grits, two huge smoked sausage patties and two butter biscuits.

People were always amazed that Tyla could put down so much food, considering her slim build. At five feet eight inches tall, she maintained her weight at one hundred and fifteen pounds by keeping physically active and horseback riding. She was the only girl and the youngest sibling in a family with three boys.

Tyla found herself in the family room, standing in front of the wall that her mother had dedicated to family pictures. Some of the photos were extremely old, like a few with her, her brothers and her brothers' best friend, Jon Jenkins, on horses. In their younger days, they went to the nearby ranch every weekend for horseback riding. Now, Tyla and her older brother, Tristen, went twice a week on Monday evenings and Saturday mornings.

She inched down a little farther until she came to a recent picture of her mother and father. Tyla still couldn't believe that her beloved father had died of a heart attack at the young age of forty-eight just three months earlier.

Her mind became filled with the account of how her parents had met. Her mother was just fourteen when she'd gotten pregnant. Not by Tyla's father though. Myah Armstrong and Maurice Jefferson didn't even know each other then. The father of Myah's baby hadn't wasted any time fleeing once she'd given him the news that they were going to have a baby. Her parents had tried to be supportive but couldn't hide the fact that she'd disappointed them immensely. Her relationship with them was never the same.

Tristen was born. He was two years old when Myah met Maurice at a rodeo in northwest Georgia where Myah lived at the time. Maurice was one of the riders from Chatta-nooga.

A slight smile tugged at the corners of Tyla's mouth as she remembered her father saying that when he saw their mother at the rodeo, he thought to himself that she could ride his horse anytime. That was when he knew he was in love because a man didn't let just anybody ride his horse. Your horse was kind of like your car. You didn't let just anybody behind the reins.

Myah was sixteen at the time and Maurice was twenty. After dating for a brief period, they got married. Maurice took his new family back with him to live in Chattanooga and adopted Tristen as his son. Not long after the couple were married, Myah became pregnant. Tristen turned three ten days before another son, Torey, was born. Three years later came one more son, Terrell. Myah never gave up her hope of having a girl one day. Two years later, Tyla was born.

After her father's sudden and unexpected death, Tyla had informed her mother that she was dropping out of modeling school in Atlanta to return home, get a part-time job and attend Chattanooga Technical School part-time in order to become a practical nurse. Her father's death had caused her to reconsider her career choice.

Forty-four-year-old Myah Jefferson strolled over and stood beside her daughter. "Good morning," Myah cheerily announced as she eased her arm around Tyla's waist and laid the side of her face against hers.

Tyla leaned into her mother. "Mornin', sleepyhead. How you doing?"

"I'm fine. How 'bout you? You rest okay?"

"Yes. I'm feeling great." Tyla took her mother's hand. "Come on. Breakfast is ready. You need to eat something."

Myah obeyed as she gave her daughter a playful warning. "I hope you know you spoilin' me."

As she stood in front of the stove with her back to her mother, Tyla spooned some grits onto a plate along with a piece of sausage and a biscuit. "So, what's wrong with that? You my momma, ain't cha?" she teased.

"Not a thing. I'm lovin' it."

Tyla brought the plate over and carefully set it on the table in front of her mother. "Here you go."

Myah looked up at her daughter and broke into a smile. "Thank you."

"You're welcome. Enjoy." Tyla leaned down and deposited a quick peck on her mother's left cheek before walking away.

Myah looked back and asked hopefully, "Aren't you gonna eat with me?"

A sheepish grin covered Tyla's face. "I'm sorry, Momma. You know me." She shrugged her shoulders. "I tried to wait on you, but—"

Myah let out a giggle. "Never mind. No need to explain."

Tyla reminded her mother, "I've got to be going. Don't want to be late my first day."

"Why don't we meet somewhere for lunch today?"

Tyla placed a hand on one hip. "Sounds good, but I've got orientation and I'm not sure what time I'll get to take lunch."

Myah frowned. "Oh, yeah. I forgot." She raised her coffee cup to her nose and breathed in the steam before taking a sip.

Tyla looked at her mother. "You go to lunch at twelve, right?"

"Yeah, but the other secretaries and I are flexible," Myah said, referring to the clerical staff in the lawyer's office where she worked. "We switch out on occasion, so when you find out what time you're getting lunch, give me a call."

"All right." Tyla turned and headed down the hallway toward her room.

Myah said a brief prayer of thanks for her food and her family. She missed Maurice so much, but having their baby girl back home again was a welcome relief.

The sky was a clear powder-blue with puffy white clouds scattered against it. The lush green vegetation of early spring standing proudly against it looked like a scene from the Tennessee calendars Tyla remembered from her childhood. It felt so good to be back home. She loved Chattanooga.

Midnight, the coal-black Tennessee walking horse she rode twice a week, trotted along the ranch's hillside path. Tyla relished her rides with Tristen. He and Marshmallow, a snow-white Arabian, followed in Midnight's tracks. Tristen was forever giving her a hard time that she got to ride the horse with the masculine name while she stuck him with Marshmallow. Tristen didn't have her fooled, though. He adored Marshmallow.

"Woo!" Tyla let out. "That was exhilarating. I could stay out here and just ride forever."

Thirty-year-old Tristen let out a hearty laugh.

"Yeah, I know. I remember what a hard time you used to give Momma and Daddy when it came time for you to get off your pony, Flash. You had the whole neighborhood thinking somebody was abusing you with all your yelling and screaming."

Tyla snickered at the memory.

They made it to the stall, dismounted their horses and handed the reins over to the groomers.

Tyla cast a smile and said, "Thank you."

"You're welcome, Miss Tyla," the young man said. "Did ju enjoy your ride?"

"Yes, I did." Tyla ignored the mock roll of her brother's eyes as she gently rubbed Midnight's shiny black coat. "Bye, Midnight. You be good. See ya later." Waving at the other horse, she added, "Bye, Marshmallow." She patted the horse as she walked away.

When they were out of earshot of the groomers, Tristen pretended to be offended as he usually did after a ride. "Did you see how he just ignored me *again?*" He imitated the groomer. "Did ju enjoy your ride, Miss Tyla?"

Tyla laughed. "You need to stop."

Tristen threw his hands to his chest. "What am I? The invisible man? They never ask if I enjoyed my ride. I guess I'll just have to ask myself." He began simulating a conversation with himself. "Mr. Tristen, did you enjoy your ride? Why, Tristen, yes, I did. Thank you for asking."

Tyla laughed harder and jabbed her brother in his side with her elbow. "Will you stop?"

As they made their way back to Tristen's Rodeo, his demeanor turned sober. "So you think you're gonna like your new job?"

"I think so. I'll just be glad when I learn everything, you know. That's the one thing I hate about starting a new job—not knowing what to do. It makes me feel like I'm not in control."

"Yeah, that's how it is when something's unfamiliar to you."

"Is that how you felt when you first became a probation officer?"

"Yeah. Even though I had the training, I didn't really learn the job till I actually started doing it. You just gotta be patient."

"Yeah, you're right. Orientation went well today. When I go in on Wednesday, they'll have one of the other registration clerks start training me. I've got school tomorrow."

"How are your classes going?"

"Pretty good. I can't wait to start doing the hands-on stuff. Gotta learn the basics first."

Tristen nodded as they walked the trail to his vehicle. "Yeah. You'll get there."

When Tristen spoke, from Tyla's point of view, he made everything in the world all right. Even though they didn't share the same biological father, neither she nor her other brothers considered him to be just their half brother. As far as they were concerned, there was nothing half about him.

Tristen was so much like their father had been and she missed him dearly. She hoped the career path she had set upon was the right choice.

Chapter 2

Despite her apathy regarding the newly hired registration clerk, Hope Mason had every intention of training her well. After all, how Tyla Jefferson performed her duties would, in part, be a reflection on Hope as her trainer.

Mercy had already hired three new part-time clerks within the past three months, all three young and childish. Hope didn't understand why they kept hiring all these immature girls who probably only took the jobs just to have spending money for clothes, hair, nails, makeup and such. She had just turned forty-eight two days ago and had three growing teenagers to take care of. She didn't need anybody else to babysit.

After Hope had introduced Tyla to the other clerks and some of the additional hospital staff, she began the tedious task of training her. She was impressed with Tyla's willingness to learn, though, and to take down handwritten notes as they went step-by-step through the patient registration process, unlike the other young clerks recently hired.

When Tyla blew out an anxious sigh, Hope asked, "What's wrong?"

Tyla kept her eyes glued to her computer screen. "This is so much information. When will I ever learn it all?"

A small portion of Hope's heart went out to Tyla. "It'll take time, but you'll learn it."

This time, Tyla looked up at her, hope shimmering in her deep brown eyes. "When? How long did it take you?"

As much as Hope opposed the hospital's decision to hire another young clerk, she didn't want to sound discouraging. But she had to be honest with her new coworker. "Within six months time, I was feeling pretty comfortable with the work and doing it on my own."

Tyla's eyes increased in size and her heartbeat quickened. "Six months?"

"That's how long it took me. It doesn't mean it'll take you that long. Everybody's different."

Tyla turned back to face her computer. "Yeah, you're right."

Hope checked her watch. "It's almost twelve. Why don't we stop here so you can take your lunch? Just log off your computer till you get back. Remember to always do that if you have to leave your station for any reason—for security purposes."

Lunch. That word was sweet music to Tyla's ears. Although she was a nervous wreck about learning this new job, she hadn't lost her appetite.

"Okay." Tyla moved the mouse over the mouse pad until the computer's arrow was where she needed it to be in order to log herself out of the program. With a couple of clicks, the computer began doing as she had instructed it. She looked at Hope. "What time do you go to lunch?"

Hope pushed back her chair and stood as she answered nonchalantly, "Usually around twelve."

Tyla's face lit up. She opened her bottom desk drawer and pulled out her pocketbook. "Oh, good. Maybe we can go together sometimes. Do you already have lunch plans for today?"

As Hope rolled her chair back toward her own station, she said, "I usually go home and eat lunch and run a few errands." She pushed her chair up to her desk and walked back over to Tyla.

Tyla said, "Oh, okay. Well, I'll be back in an hour."

Hope attempted to smile. "Okay. Enjoy your lunch."

Tyla's smile was warm. "Thanks. You, too."

Hope watched Tyla walk away and kept her attention focused on her until she rounded the corner and she could see her no longer. Tyla was very pretty. *Young* and pretty. She seemed really sweet and down-to-earth, but Hope wasn't going to let her guard down.

"So how'd it go at work today?" Tristen asked his sister as the two of them sat on the deck that evening eating supper. He was glad their mother had stepped inside the house for more corn bread and sweet tea. He'd noticed how quiet Tyla was. He sensed that she was experiencing some anxiety about something and didn't want to discuss it in their mother's presence because he didn't want her worrying about Tyla.

Tyla wiped her mouth with her napkin and placed it back on the table. "Okay."

Tristen eyed her suspiciously. "Just okay. You don't sound very enthusiastic."

Tyla returned his gaze. "It's just a lot of information to learn."

Tristen said, "Girl, it's your first week. What'd you expect?"

Tyla spoke in a low whisper. "I know that. I'm not sure about this though. Maybe I made a mistake giving up my life in Atlanta and coming back here thinking I could just dive into something new."

Tristen stared at his sister and said, "I'm shocked."

Tyla frowned and twitched her shoulders a bit. "What?"

"I'm shocked that you would say what you just did. This doesn't sound like you. The Tyla I know would be enthusiastic and positive. Besides, you're still doing your modeling part-time."

"Tristen, you don't understand. Becoming a nurse wasn't one of my goals and neither was sitting behind a desk in a hospital registering E.R. patients. Modeling was going to be my full-time career. I don't know what the heck I'm doing. I feel like I'm lost. Losing Daddy like we did made me rethink what I was doing, but I don't know now."

Tristen looked deep into his sister's eyes. Eyes that looked so much like their father's. "Tyla, whatever you do, the decision is yours. Nobody's gonna be angry with you if you decide to give up working at the hospital and training to be a nurse and return to modeling and your old job in Atlanta with BellSouth or whatever job you get. If modeling's what you want to do, then I support you one hundred percent, but you've always had such a kind, giving spirit—always reaching out to people. That's one of the things that makes you so special to me—other people, too.

"Losing Daddy was the most painful thing any of us have ever gone through. You told me yourself after he died that you wanted to take your pain and put it into helping others. I'm not trying to influence you about your decision, but how are you going to do that if you give up just like that?"

Tyla started laughing and gave her brother an evil eye. "Now that's just messed up. You take something I told you and throw it back in my face."

Tristen grinned. "That's what big brothers are for."

"Yeah, I bet you do that all the time to the kids on your caseload, don't you?"

"Sometimes. Seriously though, I'm just trying to encourage you to at least give it a little more time before you give up. I can think of a bunch of things that I almost gave up on when I first attempted them, but I didn't. Now I can look back on those experiences, and I'm glad I hung in there."

Tyla's tone grew serious. "Okay. I'm going to give it my best shot."

"I know you will," Tristen said and smiled.

The next afternoon when Tyla got out of class, she decided to walk across the street to the nearby park before going home. She loved to watch the children play. She also liked to observe the people. Not meddlesome observations but the kind that made her thirst for a better knowledge of people in general, just getting to know them.

As she took in the sights around her, Tyla pulled out a small can of smoked almonds from her book bag, removed the plastic cover and popped a nut into her mouth. In order to savor the flavor, she always ate them one by one.

While she crunched away on the nuts, a couple of pigeons flew near her and landed on the ground. She always kept a pack of crackers in her bag for the birds. She crushed a cracker and threw the pieces onto the ground. The birds strutted about, gobbling the morsels up.

Tyla watched the pigeons fly away and then decided to go home. As she was about to enter the house through the front door, she heard the beeping of a horn. When she turned around, she couldn't believe it when she saw Jon Jenkins in the driveway on a motorcycle. He climbed off the bike and removed his helmet. Tyla dropped her book bag onto the porch and ran out to greet him. As soon as she reached him, they were in each other's arms.

Since Jon was so close to her brothers, he was like another big brother to Tyla. He was twenty-nine, about a year younger than Tristen. She hadn't seen him since her father's funeral in January. The subtle fragrance of his cologne stirred her senses.

"Jon!" Tyla merrily exclaimed. "How are you?"

Jon's full lips drew into a broad grin. "I'm fine. How 'bout you?"

He couldn't take his eyes off Tyla. Her tie-dyed T-shirt, blue jeans and white sneakers, along with her hair pulled up in a ponytail, made her look like she was sixteen. She was the only girl he knew who would look good even if she wore a burlap sack. He thought back to her senior prom when he and Tristen had been her escorts. She was the prettiest girl there. He would never forget how beautiful she looked or what she wore—a very simple long, straight red dress with spaghetti straps and a sash draped around her neck, and matching red sandals.

Ever since Jon had seen Tyla at her father's funeral, he hadn't been able to get her off his mind. She'd always been like his little sister, but suddenly he'd started looking at her differently. She was a woman now. A very attractive one. Not just on the outside but on the inside.

"I'm good," Tyla cheerfully responded. It's great seeing you again. So how are your parents? Momma said they moved to Florida recently."

They stood facing each other, holding hands and grinning like two Cheshire cats.

"Yeah. They're fine. Enjoying all that Florida sunshine. Tristen told me you moved back home with your mom. He said you're going to Chattanooga Tech to be a nurse and working at Mercy."

"Yeah. Nursing's my calling now, but I'm still modeling part-time."

"That's good. I know how much you enjoy modeling. So what have they got you doing at Mercy?"

"I'm an E.R. registration clerk."

"That's great. Do you like it?"

"Well, the verdict's still out on that question. I'm not sure yet. I just started Monday and spent the entire day in orientation. I go to school on Tuesdays and Thursdays. Yesterday, at the hospital, I actually got to sit at the computer and had some training on how to register the patients who come into the E.R. So I haven't really gotten my feet wet yet. I kind of feel like I'm standing on shore watching everybody else swim."

Jon nodded. He and Tyla finally let go of each other's hands.

He kindly offered, "Anytime you're learning something new, you're going to feel that way. I know you. It won't be long before you'll have that computer smoking you'll be registering those patients so fast."

Tyla dropped her head and leaned over as she laughed. Jon reminded her of Tristen. They both always knew how to make her feel better.

She looked at the bike. "When'd you get the motorcycle?"

Jon grinned proudly. "A few weeks ago. You wanna ride?"

Tyla's eyes lit up. "Sure. Let's go inside for a few minutes first. I know Momma would love to see you." As they made their way toward the house, she asked, "So what are you up to these days?"

"Mostly working."

"Are you still in engineering?"

Jon nodded. "Yes."

"Biomedical, right?"

Jon nodded several times. "You got it." He was impressed that she remembered.

As they entered the living room, Tyla yelled, "Momma! Guess who's here! Come into the living room!"

They sat on the sofa.

While they waited for Myah to appear, Tyla asked, "So are you still working at the university?"

"Yes, but I hope to be leaving soon."

"Really? Why? Don't you like it?"

"Yeah, I love it. I don't want to leave my field of study. I just want a change. I would love to work in a hospital."

Tyla nodded. "You do prosthetics, too, don't you?"

"Yes."

"That must be rewarding in itself."

"It is," Jon agreed. "To give people a new lease on life by replacing a missing part of their body makes me feel good."

Tyla smiled. "That's wonderful, Jon. I'm so happy for you. So have you checked with any of the hospitals here in Chattanooga to see what's available in your field?"

His smile ignited a twinkle in his eyes. "Yeah, as a matter of fact, I had a job interview this morning at Mercy."

Tyla's whole face began to glow. "Wow! That's great. How did it go?"

"It went good. I think I've got the job. They have a few more people to interview, but they said I'm in their list of top candidates."

"That's terrific." Tyla stood. "Would you excuse me for a moment? Let me see if I can find Momma. She should be here. Her car's outside."

"Sure." Jon nodded.

Tyla headed down the hallway, yelling, "Momma!"

Suddenly, Jon heard another female voice say, "I'm coming. I was in the bathroom."

He heard Tyla say, "Jon's here."

Then he saw Myah appear with an embarrassed look on her face. "Jon!" she screamed. As she made her way to him, she fussed at her daughter. "Tyla, you got me yellin' my business for all to hear and we got company."

Tyla followed her mother. She let out a snort as she said, "Jon's not company. He's part of the family."

Tyla's words were a tender caress. Jon stood and walked with arms outstretched toward Myah. "Mrs. J."

They threw their arms around each other. Myah sat down and the three of them talked for several minutes.

Tyla rose. "Momma, Jon's gonna take me for a ride on his motorcycle."

Jon got up from his seat.

Myah's jubilation tumbled like dominoes collapsing. Her piercing eyes looked up at Tyla and Jon. "Motorcycle? What motorcycle?"

Tyla pulled her mother up by the hand. "The one in our driveway that he recently bought." She led Myah outside as Jon followed.

Myah knit her eyebrows together. "I don't know, Tyla. Motorcycles are dangerous."

"They're not any more dangerous than cars," Tyla countered.

Jon assured Myah, "I'll take care of her, Mrs. J."

Myah trusted Jon like she did her own children. Nevertheless, she was reluctant and cautioned them to be careful as she watched them put on their helmets and climb onto the motorcycle.

Jon turned the cycle around in the driveway and eased out onto the road. Myah thought she would pass out as she watched them take off with Tyla screaming excitedly. God knew what he was doing when he'd given her only one girl like Tyla. Another tomboyish girl would have really put Myah on edge.

As she headed back toward the house, she grumbled, "Lord, that girl's gonna be the death of me."

Chapter 3

Tyla felt herself getting more and more frustrated. All the training in the world wasn't going to help her learn this job. What had she been thinking? She must have been crazy to have given up her job at BellSouth in Atlanta where she had worked full-time for the past three and a half years before she'd decided to go to modeling school. Her supervisor had been kind enough to switch her to part-time and had even set her work hours around her school schedule. Perhaps she hadn't thought everything through before making her decision.

To make matters worse, Hope had had some sort of family emergency and wouldn't be coming in until sometime later in the day. LaPorsha Dupree, the thirty-five-year-old big mouth who was training Tyla in Hope's absence, was driving Tyla up the wall.

One of the first things out of LaPorsha's mouth before

she even uttered good morning was something negative about Hope's personality. When Tyla had refused to comment, LaPorsha had just come flat out and asked her what she thought of Hope.

Tyla had told LaPorsha that she thought Hope was nice. Then LaPorsha had said that in due time, Tyla would see Hope's true personality. The last thing Tyla wanted was to be involved in any office gossip about her coworkers or anyone else. She couldn't wait for Hope to get back and take over her training.

LaPorsha said, "Tabitha said she heard you ask Hope if she wanted to go to lunch with you when you were here Wednesday, but she wouldn't go."

Tabitha Peavy was another registration clerk. She was sixty years old.

Tyla uttered a brief silent prayer asking God to help her respond in a kind manner to LaPorsha's comments. "All I did was ask her if she had plans for lunch and she said she usually goes home for lunch and runs errands. It wasn't a big deal."

LaPorsha leaned in a little closer to Tyla and attempted to whisper. "Well, don't hold your breath. She ain't gon' go to lunch with you. When she first came here, we tried to be nice to her. We were always inviting her to lunch and trying to get her involved with things we were doing. But she always had her nose up in the air like she was better than us or something. Finally, I just said, to heck with her. If she wanna act like that, let her. Ain't no skin off my back. She's weird. I don't know why she acts like that. She must have some really serious issues."

Tyla had heard enough. "LaPorsha, I'm not trying to be ugly, but I want to learn my job. Can you please just teach me how to do it? I'm here to work. Everybody's got issues. I could care less about Hope and her—"

Before Tyla could finish her sentence, a voice from behind them hissed, "If you've got something to say about me, I'd appreciate it if you'd say it to my face."

Tyla turned around to face Hope, but LaPorsha dared not look back.

Tyla uttered, "Excuse me?"

Hope said, "You heard me. I didn't stutter."

Tyla said, "Hope, I wasn't talking about—"

Hope put up her hand. "Save it. I'm here to train you. We have to work together, but we don't have to be friends."

Tyla's mouth fell open. "Why are you mad at me? I wasn't talking about you."

"I know what I heard."

"You didn't hear what you think you did." Tyla cast a brief glance at LaPorsha, her eyes pleading for the woman to come to her defense.

Tyla had just started this job and was having enough trouble as it was learning what to do and getting adjusted. She didn't need her coworker and trainer, or anybody else, angry at her, especially not over some misunderstanding.

LaPorsha kept her eyes glued to the computer screen and didn't say a word. Tyla wanted to slap the look off her face. She considered telling Hope everything LaPorsha had said about her. But instead, she let the accusation stay where it was—on her.

Hope said, "LaPorsha, thanks for covering for me. I'll pick up where you left off."

LaPorsha got up from the seat and rushed from the station like a streak of lightning. Hope trained Tyla up until they stopped for lunch. Afterward, they picked up where they left off, but the tension in the air was so thick that it would have taken a chain saw to cut it.

Later that evening, Jon took Tyla to one of her favorite restaurants, Waffle House. He didn't know any woman who was more down-to-earth than she was. She was quiet tonight, though, very much unlike her. At first, he'd thought it was his imagination. However, when he saw her plate still piled high with her food several minutes after the waitress had brought it out, he knew he wasn't mistaken.

He looked her square in her face. "Something's bothering you." His tone was filled with kindness.

Tyla batted her eyes a couple of times. For a few seconds, it seemed that she and Jon were the only two people in the restaurant. "What gave me away?"

When he pointed at her plate, they both broke out in laughter.

He said, "I don't think I've ever seen you *not* have an appetite. All the years we've known each other, I've never seen it."

Her laughter subsided. Her expression was still troubled but less melancholy. "Yeah, I guess there's a first time for everything. This is one for the record books."

"Do you want to talk about it?"

Tyla heaved a heavy sigh. "This morning at work, Hope, my coworker who's training me, had an emergency at home. So one of our other coworkers had to train me till she got there. Anyway, the lady who was training me in her place was saying all these negative things about her. She was saying Hope is weird and must really have some serious issues. I tried not to be rude, but I finally asked her to just train me to do my job. I told her everybody has issues. Then I started to tell her I could care less about Hope and hers. Well, Hope walked in at just that moment and thought *I* was the one bad-mouthing her behind her back."

"Did you try to explain to her what actually happened?" Jon's tone was serious yet filled with tenderness.

"Not exactly. I let her believe I was the one doing the bad-mouthing."

"What did the other woman say—the one who was doing all the negative talking?"

Tyla released a fake chuckle. "Nothing. She just sat there like a knot on a log, looking all crazy."

Jon reached across the table and gave her hand a quick stroke. "Tyla, you've got to defend yourself. You can't let people do you like that."

Tyla looked away. "I just started this job. It's stressful enough trying to learn everything they want me to do. I don't want to be caught up in the middle of any bickering on top of it."

Jon looked at Tyla, his eyes unwavering. "Sounds like you already are."

She looked at him and held his gaze. "Yeah, I guess you're right."

"So what are you going to do about it?"

"I don't know. I have the weekend to think it over and pray about it."

"Yeah, you do that."

Tyla cast him a smile. "Thanks for listening."

"Anytime."

Her anxiety having melted away, Tyla suddenly sat up straight in her seat. "Excuse me." She bowed her head and said a brief, silent prayer of thanks for her food before digging in.

Jon grinned. "Welcome back."

Tyla blushed.

He sipped his tea, and they talked while they ate.

"I've got some good news," Jon said.

"Really? Tell me." Tyla popped another piece of grilled pork chop in her mouth and chewed while she waited.

Jon's face was radiant. "I got the job."

Tyla opened her eyes wide. She wiped her mouth with her paper napkin and laid it beside her plate. "The one at Mercy?"

Jon nodded. "Yeah."

"Yeah!" Tyla exclaimed. "So when do you start?"

"In two weeks."

Tyla smiled. "That's great. I am so happy for you. Tonight, dinner's on me."

Jon shook his head. "Oh, no. I asked you out."

"I know, but you just landed the job you wanted. You've got to let me do this. You'd do it for me." Placing her hand gently on his arm, she pleaded, "Please, Jon, let me do it. I want to."

Jon felt a fluttering in his stomach. Butterflies. He hadn't felt them for anyone in a long while. Finally, he said, "Okay. Thank you."

"You're welcome. Congratulations."

They went to see a movie after dinner. When Jon took Tyla home, it was almost midnight. He came inside for a few minutes. Myah was still up, so he got a chance to talk with her. As soon as he left, Tyla went to bed. As she lay there and thought about him, she was aware of a warm, funny feeling in the pit of her stomach. Butterflies.

Chapter 4

Tristen was going to great lengths to keep the family together since his father's death. After the funeral, he had called a family meeting and told everyone that family gatherings were something they needed to do, not just during the holidays but on a regular basis in order to keep their family connected. Everybody had agreed that they would all meet at Momma's on the last Sunday of each month for family fellowshipping.

Today was the last Sunday in April. Twenty-seven-year-old Torey and his wife, Michelle, had traveled from their hometown of Ringgold, Georgia, which was about thirty minutes south of Chattanooga. The youngest brother, twenty-four-year-old Terrell, had come from his home in Chattanooga. His girlfriend, Olivia McDonald, who also lived nearby in Chattanooga, had accompanied him.

Tyla had helped her mother prepare the main dishes the

day before to go with the ones that everyone else would be bringing to the table. Therefore, when the two women had come home after morning worship service, all they had to do was remove the food from the refrigerator and start the heating process. By the time the rest of the family had arrived, everything was piping hot.

After dinner, they sat around talking.

Tyla tilted her head to one side. "Guess what? I bumped into Jon the other day."

Terrell asked, "How's he doing? I haven't seen or talked to him since the funeral."

Tyla cheerily replied, "He's great. He just accepted a job at Mercy. You know he's a biomedical engineer."

Myah noticed the way her daughter's eyes twinkled when she spoke of Jon. It was the same sparkle people had accused Myah of having when she'd met Maurice. Had Tyla fallen in love?

Terrell responded, "Yeah, I remember. That's great."

Tyla said, "Why don't you come with me and Tristen and Jon to the ranch sometime and go riding with us?"

Terrell replied, "It's been a while since I rode. I probably don't even remember what to do."

Tyla shot him a pointed look. "I don't believe that. Riding a horse is just like riding a bicycle. Once you learn, you never forget."

Torey took his sister's comment as his opportunity to dive into the conversation. He grinned and spoke loud above the buzz of noise in the family room where they were sitting.

Referring to his sister by the childhood nickname he'd

given her, Torey said, "Baby girl, that's your philosophy for everything. Just like people saying all exotic meat tastes like chicken when they know good and well it don't."

Laughter filled the air.

Tyla came back at Torey. "You better hush before I come over there and put a hurting on you."

"In your dreams," Torey hollered back.

Tyla looked at her sister-in-law. "Michelle, you need to get your husband."

Michelle said, "Honey, he's yours now. I have to deal with him at home three hundred and sixty-five days a year. Now it's your turn."

Everybody burst into laughter again.

Tyla teased, "Hey, you married him. So he's your problem now. Don't be trying to put him off on me."

Michelle was laughing so hard that she almost fell out of her seat onto the floor. "Girl, you a mess. A true mess."

Tyla looked at twenty-two-year-old Olivia. "Olivia, what you laughing at? You're stuck with this one here." She pointed her thumb toward her brother Terrell, who was sitting beside her.

Terrell fell out laughing. "Wait a minute, now. How you gon' throw down on me? I wasn't even saying anything."

Tyla said, "Well, I thought I'd get you one good time before you get started. Besides, I'm sure I owe you that one plus some more from when we were kids. You were always doing something to aggravate me. Now it's payback time."

Myah exclaimed, "See what y'all did? You created a monster. I told you she was gonna end up just like all three of you."

Tristen said, "Oh, Momma, please. Tyla had you fooled. She had you thinking she was your little angel when she was anything but. As soon as your back was turned, she was getting into something and you'd blame us."

Myah said, "Well, she imitated everything she saw y'all do so it was probably something she picked up from you anyway."

Through their laughter, they heard the doorbell.

Tyla jumped up. She had an idea who it was. "I'll get it." She made her way to the front door. When she opened it, there he was. The man who gave her butterflies.

"Jon!" Tyla exclaimed. "I'm so glad you could make it. Come in. The whole gang's here."

Jon followed her into the family room where he gave everyone a hug, including the guys. Everybody here was family.

As Tyla stole glimpses here and there of Jon interacting with her family, she saw him in a completely different light. She wondered if he was feeling the same way about her.

Hope made a final check of the time on the sunflower-shaped clock on the wall beside the stove.

"Okay, guys, you gotta hurry up or you'll miss the bus. And I don't have time to take you to school this morning. I've got an early morning meeting at work. And don't forget I'm working this evening at the store till ten." She was referring to her part-time job at the Main Junction. "You can have leftovers from yesterday for supper."

Her three teenagers stayed in their seats as though their bottoms were glued to them. Hope walked toward them, her hands moving frantically in an upward motion. "Come on. Hop to it."

Her eldest child and only son, sixteen-year-old Brandon, mumbled as he pulled himself from his chair. "Well, if you'd get me a car, I could drive us to school."

Hope did not want to have this argument with him this morning. With the children's father behind in his child-support payments, she could barely keep her head above water as it was.

"Brandon, don't start that again. I told you we can't afford a car for you right now."

Fourteen-year-old Ashlee and thirteen-year-old Brittney got up from the table and went in the direction of their shared bedroom, leaving their brother to his debate with their mother.

The tall, slim, dark-eyed teenager who looked too much like his deceitful father announced, "I can get a part-time job after school and buy my own car."

"Your grades have already slipped this school year. You're barely making Cs. You need to spend your time studying. Besides, you can't make enough money to buy a car working part-time."

"I'll ask Dad to help me pay for it."

Hope hated to burst her son's bubble. She'd kept secret from the children how lax her ex-husband, Lance Harris, was regarding his child-support payments. As much as she hated him and her ex-best friend, Leeza, whom he'd left her for and married, she wanted her children to have a relation-ship with him.

Hope's voice filled with sternness and rose an octave. "I told you, no car. You just concentrate on bringing your grades up."

Brandon started to say something but held back when he saw the look on his mother's face. Instead, he went to get his book bag from his room. A few minutes later, he and his sisters returned.

Hope started bidding each of them farewell. She told Ashlee and Brittney, "Have a good day. See you this evening when I get home from work." Looking at her son's head, she asked, "Brandon, did you brush your hair?"

The older teenager mumbled, "Yeah."

Hope leaned back, her eyes wide. "Excuse me."

"Yes," Brandon murmured.

Hope vigorously rubbed her right hand over his head. "You sure? It doesn't look like it. Go brush it again. I don't want you going to school with your head looking like you just got outta bed."

Without uttering a word, the boy quickly walked back toward his room.

When he returned, his mother smiled and said, "That's better. Now was that so bad?"

Brandon turned up the corners of his mouth and tried not to roll his eyes.

When Hope attempted to peck his cheek, he quickly moved and muttered, "I gotta go."

Disappointment and hurt washed over Hope's soul as she stood in the breeze left by Brandon's sudden rush to catch the bus. "'Bye. Have a good day!" she yelled just as the front door slammed shut.

Hope strolled over to the love seat next to the living room window, plopped down on it and watched her teenagers as they waited for their bus. It seemed like yesterday that all three of them were just babies. She and Lance had wanted three children, all close in age. After Brandon, she'd had a difficult time conceiving Ashlee, which explained the nearly two-year age difference. Ashlee was just three months old when Hope had gotten pregnant with Brittney.

Hadn't she and Lance been happy together? Hope had thought they were until she'd found the letters Leeza had written him. Leeza. Her best friend. The one who had been there for them during the births of all three of their children. Had babysat for them. Came to their home and ate with them. Invited them to her house and shared meals with them. Hope soon found out that hadn't been all she'd shared.

Hope had been there for Leeza when Leeza's own husband had left her for another woman. Then the friend she'd loved like a sister betrayed her like an enemy. And now, look at what her and Lance's deception had done to Hope's family. The girls seemed to be handling the divorce all right, but poor Brandon, who used to be so outgoing, had shut down. He was a young boy who needed his father on a full-time basis, but Lance and Leeza's selfishness had destroyed their lives forever.

Hope attempted to keep her tears at bay but wasn't successful. She watched her children climb onto the bus and kept the vehicle in view until she could see it no more.

* * *

Tyla was elated that the meeting had only lasted an hour. All the talk about policy and procedure had overwhelmed her. How were they supposed to learn all this stuff, let alone remember it? As the staff made their way to their workstations, she tried to make light conversation with Hope.

"How was your weekend?"

No one ever asked Hope about her weekend. She was still angry at Tyla for talking about her to LaPorsha and wished she'd stop trying to talk to her. "Fine. Why?" Her tone was not a pleasant one.

Tyla smiled. "I was just wondering if you had a nice one." She pulled open her bottom desk drawer and deposited her purse before taking her seat.

When Hope joined Tyla in her work area, Tyla could still feel the hostility reeking from the woman. Tyla had talked to her family about the situation and everyone had been encouraging, except for Terrell. He'd advised her to stop trying to make Hope like her and tell her to go jump in a lake and cool off. He hadn't been serious. But even though he was just cutting up, their mother had severely chastised him.

Hope was talking in a robotic tone. "Do a patient search first by the patient's social security number, then by the patient's name and date of birth. If the patient has any previous visits, the information will be displayed."

Tyla was finding it hard to concentrate, although she was taking her usual notes on the legal pad in front of her.

Hope rattled on. "Verify the patient's identity by asking for their full legal name, social security number and date of birth."

Tyla tried to pay close attention as Hope spit out additional information for several more minutes.

Finally, Tyla asked, "Can we stop a minute?"

Perturbation was scrawled across Hope's face. "Why? What's wrong?"

Tyla placed her elbow on her desk and rubbed her forehead with her fingers. Facing Hope, she asked, "Can we talk a minute?"

Hope's expression remained frozen. "About what?"

Tyla placed her hands in her lap and offered her coworker a look filled with sincerity. "Hope, I think we got off to a bad start. What you think was happening last week when you walked in, wasn't. I know that's how it sounded and I guess if I were you, I would've thought the same thing, but that's not how it was. Can we start fresh? I have to work with you and everybody else here. I don't want any animosity between us."

Hope wasn't letting down her guard. That's how she'd gotten hurt in the past—being too trusting. And the very ones who'd betrayed her had been her friends. She had always tried to be a true friend. Had gone out of her way to be there for people. And the one time she needed someone to be there for her, all she'd gotten was stabbed in the back. The only person she could depend on was herself. She didn't need anyone else.

Inasmuch as she needed the child-support money that Lance was behind in paying, she was determined to show him, too, that she didn't need him, which was why she'd gotten the part-time job at the Junction, as the local people called it. It took every ounce of what little energy she had left to put in more hours after having worked at Mercy. She didn't need any more *so-called* friends in her life to let her down again.

Hope firmly stated, "Listen. We don't have to be friends. We just have to work together. You don't have to like me and I don't have to like you. The only reason I'm here is to earn a paycheck so I can take care of my kids."

Tyla had never known anyone with Hope's pessimistic views. "What's wrong with being nice to people?"

Hope looked at Tyla. "You are so young and naive."

Tyla almost lost her cool. Some people treated her as though she were dumb just because she was young. "Maybe I am young, but I'm not naive. I just believe in being kind to people."

Hope let out a fake chuckle. "That's the kind of thinking that'll get you burned."

Tyla stared in disbelief at her coworker, her mouth open. "How can you say that?"

Hope responded without hesitation. "That's just the way it is. Live a little longer. You'll see."

"Listen. I just want us to be friends."

"I don't need any more friends," Hope snapped. "Can we get back to work?"

Tyla didn't say anything. How could anyone be so bitter? She couldn't work in this kind of environment and decided immediately to put in for a transfer to another department.

Chapter 5

Tristen checked his watch as he made his way up the driveway of his client's home. Having recently received a youth from out of state on his caseload, he had to make a home visit to check out the family's living situation and see if it was acceptable for the youth. While the youth was in school, Tristen could meet the parents and check out the home before the father had to leave for work. It was almost eleven-thirty. He had just enough time to talk with the parents and get a walk-through of the house before meeting Tyla for lunch at twelve.

Tristen had parked his Rodeo on the side of the yard. He didn't like pulling into people's driveways and risking the chance of having someone pull in behind him and boxing him in. The safety training his office had attended recently made him even more aware of the need to continue his routine in case he ever ran into danger and had to make a quick exit.

He had made it about halfway up the driveway when out

of the corner of his right eye, he caught sight of something coming rapidly toward him. Tristen quickly looked to his right. In a neighbor's yard, approximately forty feet from him, was the biggest Doberman pinscher he'd ever seen coming straight at him.

Tristen felt his heart thumping against his chest like the beating of a drum as his mind raced with as many things as he could remember from the training on what to do and not do in order to prevent dog attacks.

It was all going through his head as though someone had pressed the fast-forward button on a DVD player. He had no idea that his brain could execute stored data that quickly. *Stay in your car.* Too late—he was already out of his vehicle. *Don't run and avoid eye contact. If attacked, fall onto the ground, curl up into a ball and protect your head, neck and face with your arms and yell for help.*

Fall onto the ground and be attacked. Are they for real? I'm getting my behind outta here.

The animal was gaining speed as it raced toward Tristen. Tristen turned on his heels, aimed his remote at the passenger side door of his Rodeo, pressed the unlock button and took off running across his client's yard toward the vehicle.

Tristen hadn't noticed the huge rosebush at the driveway's edge as he'd walked up the entrance, but here it was. And he could do one of two things. Slow his pace and run around it or— Before he could get his last thought out, he had lifted himself up into the air and jumped over the bush. A few more steps and his hand was on the door handle of the Rodeo. Just as he got the passenger door open, he felt something tugging on his right pant leg. He kicked his right foot back as hard as he could and slammed the door shut.

With his heart pounding up against his chest, Tristen stared out the window to see the Doberman standing outside barking at the top of its lungs. Glancing down at his right leg, he saw where some fabric was missing from the bottom of his pants where the dog had gotten hold of it.

He looked out the window again and saw a man coming from the house he'd been headed to. Tristen watched the man take the animal by its collar and attempt to calm it down. He inserted his keys into the ignition and turned it slightly. Then he let down the passenger side window just enough for him and the man to communicate.

The man said, "Are you Mr. Jefferson, Tristen Jefferson, the juvenile probation officer?"

Tristen attempted to catch his breath as he replied, "Yeah."

The man introduced himself as the out-of-state youth's father. "This is our neighbor's dog. They keep him on a chain. He must've gotten loose."

Tristen replied through the crack in the window. "Yeah, I guess he did. He scared the mess outta me."

"He won't hurt you. Did you run?"

Tristen let out a sound somewhere between a snicker and a snort. "Of course I ran. He was chasing me."

"The only reason he kept coming after you was because you ran."

"Well, next time, I'll just stand there and wait for him to stop and shake hands with him and introduce myself."

The man laughed from his belly. "I'll take him back

home. You can get out now. My wife's here." He nodded toward his house. "I'll be back in a minute."

Tristen looked at the house and saw a woman standing on the porch. "I'll just wait here till you take Cujo home and make sure he's back on his chain."

The man laughed again. "You're funny. Our son's probation officer in California didn't have much of a sense of humor. Always had a frown on his face."

"Well, some people take their jobs very seriously," was all Tristen could think to say.

The man nodded. "Well, I'll be back in a minute." As he guided the dog back toward its domain, he said, "Come on, Tiny, let's go home."

Tristen mouthed *Tiny*, turned up the corners of his mouth and shook his head.

Tyla's watch read 12:06 p.m. Tristen had called her at the hospital to tell her that he needed to go home and change his pants before meeting her for lunch. She'd told him that she didn't have time for him to do that and to just come on. He'd sounded out of breath and she hadn't gotten any more than that from him. She hoped everything was okay.

Catching sight of him in his black Rodeo in her rearview mirror as she sat waiting for him in the Wendy's parking lot, she hopped out of her Volkswagen bug as he whipped into the space to the right of her.

As Tristen made his way over to her, Tyla asked, "What happened? Why'd you need to go home and change pants?" They embraced.

Tristen glanced down at his right leg and chuckled, "I got into a fight with a dog. He ripped my pants."

Shock and fear rippled through Tyla's body as she looked down at her brother's pants. Now she understood why he'd wanted to go home and change. Her brother had a thing about neatness—his dress and grooming, his house—everything had to be spotless and in place. She and their family constantly teased him that it was the reason he couldn't keep a woman for too long.

She stared him square in the face. "What happened?"

Tristen placed his hand on the small of her back to gently urge her along toward the entrance of the restaurant. "I was making a home visit on one of my clients. A neighbor's dog came running at me."

Tyla threw her right hand to her mouth. "Oh, my God. Are you all right?"

Tristen released another chuckle. "I'm here to tell you about it, ain't I?"

As they made their way into the restaurant, Tyla said, "You know, you really need to find a different job. You never know when you're gonna be shot at, chased by dogs and only God knows what else."

They got in line.

Tristen chuckled again. "That can happen no matter what profession you're in. As a matter of fact, it can happen when you're just walking down the street minding your own business."

Tyla knew her brother was right, but her heart cringed at the thought of anything terrible happening to him. They chatted while they waited for the man in front of them to finish placing his order.

Suddenly, they heard the man yelling at the cashier, "You tryin' to cheat me or somethin'? I gave you a ten. You owe me five more dollars. Can't you add and subtract?"

Tyla rolled her eyes at the man as she elbowed Tristen's arm and whispered, "Listen to that jerk. That's uncalled for—talking to that poor girl like that."

Tristen stepped in front of his sister and whispered, "Be cool."

Tyla uttered, "Don't be telling me to be cool. Tell that jerk in front of you."

The frightened girl at the register looked no more than sixteen years old. Since it was the middle of a school day, Tyla wondered if she was a high school dropout, on a work-release program from school, or perhaps a little older than she looked. Regardless, it made her so angry to witness how some folks talked to young people who were working trying to earn an honest living for themselves.

The girl apologized through tears and offered the man a five-dollar bill, which he snatched from her hand.

Tyla felt her blood boiling. As she and Tristen placed their orders, she could see the man standing to the left of them, waiting on his order. *The jerk.* Tristen was making an effort to keep himself between the man and his sister. He knew Tyla's mouth when it came to defending others.

Tyla's heart went out to the cashier. When she gave Tristen his change after he'd paid for their lunch, she attempted to smile at them through her tears.

Tyla returned her smile and said in a friendly, sincere tone, hoping the jackass beside them would hear, "You're doing a good job. It's okay. Some folks are just bullies and don't care how they talk to people. Keep your chin up."

Tristen was uttering two prayers: one, that his sister would keep quiet and say no more, and two, that the man wasn't one of those people who pulled out a gun and started shooting up the place. He knew where Tyla's heart was and he admired her genuine concern for people. But many times a person's sincere efforts to come to another person's aid had cost the life of the individual trying to help.

The cashier smiled graciously and mumbled, "Thank you."

The man glared at Tristen and Tyla. Casting his glance back at Tristen, he said, "You better tell your woman to keep her mouth shut and mind her own business."

People in line had horrified looks on their faces as they witnessed the exchange that was about to take place between Tristen and the man.

Tristen respectfully replied, "Sir, we're not trying to start any trouble here. She's not my woman. She's my sister. She was just trying to make the young lady feel better. You can understand that, can't you? You wouldn't want anybody screaming at your mother, wife, daughter or sister, would you? I've already been chased and almost mauled by a dog today. My sister and I just came in here to enjoy a meal together. That's all."

The scowl on the man's face told Tristen that he was about to really go ballistic. The beat of Tristen's heart against his chest was pounding in his ears.

Suddenly, the man's look of scorn turned to one of remorse. To everyone's surprise, he looked at the cashier he'd yelled at and said, "Miss, I'm sorry for yelling at you. You look like you might be my daughter's age and the man's right. I wouldn't want anybody yelling at her."

The cashier whispered, "Thank you."

The man retrieved his tray of food from the counter and walked away. The thumping in Tristen's chest began to wane.

As they waited on their food, Tristen whispered to Tyla, "Girl, you gon' get us killed. And you're worried about me getting shot on my job and being chased by dogs. Your mouth is what's gon' get me killed."

Tyla whispered back, "Well, I couldn't just stand here and not say anything."

"Uh-huh," was all Tristen would say.

Tyla didn't know what she would've done if her brother hadn't been there to calm the man down. She thanked God for her brother and the outcome of the situation.

The excitement in the restaurant from earlier having calmed down, Tyla and Tristen were finally able to enjoy their lunch.

Tyla was saying, "She was telling me stuff like we don't have to be friends and we don't have to like each other. I've never met anybody like her before. She sounds so bitter." She continued to ignore the fact that her brother had looked at his right pant leg several times during the course of the conversation.

Tristen offered, "Maybe she's been through something traumatic and it left a bad taste in her mouth."

Tyla scooped up some ketchup on a French fry and popped it into her mouth. "What can a person possibly go through that can make them like that?"

Tristen looked at his sister. She was smart, but in a lot of ways, she still looked at the world through rose-colored glasses. "Tyla, you're young and—"

Tyla glared at him. "Don't you start that crap with me, too. I'm tired of everybody referring to how young I am. Just because I'm young, it doesn't mean I'm dumb."

Tristen held up one hand in an effort to call a truce. "Hey, don't bite my head off. I've already almost lost it twice today. Remember?"

"Well, I didn't mean to go off on you. I'm just so tired of everybody acting like I don't know anything because of my age. You're just eight years older than me and people don't treat you this way."

Tristen reminded his sister, "I'm thirty. You're twenty-two. I'm an ole man, remember?" He smiled and put a spoonful of his chocolate Frosty into his mouth.

Tyla grinned. "I know I'm always calling you an ole man, but you know I'm only joking when I say it."

"I know. I was just messin' with you. Listen. If this woman doesn't want to be your friend, you can't force yourself on her. Give her space if that's what she wants. Friendships take time."

"But I've always been able to instantly become friends with people," Tyla protested.

"Well, everybody's not the same. For some people, it just takes longer for a friendship to develop. I predict that one day you and this lady will be the best of friends."

"I don't know. She's pretty tough."

"I know you don't see it now, but I'm telling you, it's going to happen."

Tyla looked at her brother. "How do you know?"

"Well, you just said it yourself a minute ago. You have the ability to instantly make friends with people."

Tyla rolled her eyes at Tristen. "I said *instantly.*"

Tristen laughed. "You've only been working there a week."

Tyla's jovial mood had returned, and she laughed. Checking her watch, she said, "I better be going."

Tristen looked at his watch. "Me, too."

They stood.

Tyla asked, "See you tonight?" She always looked forward to her horseback rides with her brother.

"Yeah. Same place. Same time."

"Okay." She reached for her tray.

"I'll get it. You go on."

Tyla smiled inside as she watched her brother meticulously wipe off their table with a leftover napkin.

"Thanks." Tyla pecked Tristen's cheek before trekking out the door.

Tristen threw away their trash, put up their trays and left the restaurant. His next stop was to be at one of the local high schools to visit a couple of his clients. Hopefully, there would be no dogs on the premises.

Chapter 6

Hope's shift started at six. As she sat in the Junction parking lot in her twelve-year-old navy-blue Honda Accord, she glanced at her wristwatch. Five-thirteen. She could get at least a thirty-minute nap before she went inside to start her shift. But she couldn't really go to sleep. She might not wake up in time. She was so sleepy. Her eyelids were getting heavy.

Hope tried to ignore the pounding sound in her dream. *Stop!* she demanded, but she couldn't make it quit. She opened her eyes and saw a man on the driver's side of her car, leaning down and knocking on the window with his fist. Her doors were locked. The weather was warm, so she had left about a two-inch crack in her window to keep air in and criminals out.

The man yelled, "Are you okay?"

Hope felt misplaced. She couldn't remember where she

was or what day it was until she focused her eyes and stared off into the distance at the huge sign over the Junction store looming ahead of her. She looked at her watch. It was almost six-thirty.

The man yelled again, "Are you okay?"

Hope shouted through the window's small opening, "I'm fine," and quickly rolled up her window. Without saying another word, she started the car's engine and drove away, leaving the man standing there.

Not knowing who the man was, she hadn't wanted to exit her vehicle so close to him and had crossed over to the opposite side of the parking lot. She parked her Honda, jumped out and raced to the store.

She was so embarrassed. She'd never been late for either of her jobs without first calling ahead and letting them know. She took pride in her promptness. She could kick herself for falling asleep. Then it dawned on her that the man knocking on her car window must have thought that she was sick, injured or, worse, dead, and had stopped to check on her. She felt a little guilty for leaving him standing there like she had. Perhaps there were still some decent human beings left in the world. She quickly dismissed the thought from her mind because it was that kind of gullible thinking that got you hurt.

Hope opened her left eye, half squinting at the digital clock on her bedside table. She couldn't believe she'd slept until almost noon, but then again, she wasn't all that surprised. Working both a full- and part-time job and trying to raise three teenagers were taking a toll on her physically, mentally and emotionally.

As perturbed as she was at Lance for being behind on his child-support payments, when he'd called her at the hospital yesterday, she'd agreed to allow the children to spend the weekend with him and Leeza. Now she was glad she had. Friday nights were usually busy with Brandon playing high school football and the girls performing in the band at the game.

So far, Hope had allowed Brandon to remain on the team despite his low grades. She didn't want to deny him this privilege that he thoroughly enjoyed, especially since he was having such a difficult time adjusting to his father's absence.

Every time Hope saw her ex-husband and ex-best friend together, it made her blood boil. If it wasn't for the children, she'd just pack up all her belongings and move someplace else, thousands of miles away from the two of them. After the divorce, she had casually mentioned moving to the kids, but they had not been thrilled with the idea.

Sleeping until noon made Hope wish she could afford to buy Brandon a decent cheap used car so he could drive himself and his sisters where they needed to go. However, the thought suddenly occurred to her that if she could, she'd never be able to rest for worrying about them being in a tragic accident. Every time she turned on the news, she was hearing about a bunch of teenagers getting killed in car crashes. She worried so much about her children and what would become of them if something ever happened to her.

Neither Lance nor Leeza nor anybody else would take care of them like she did.

Hope was proud of the fact that she was taking care of all their needs, despite how fatigued she always felt. Well, all their needs but one. She thought for a moment. When was the last time she and the children had been to church together? Over a year. Occassionally, the kids would go with some of their friends. As for herself, she was too busy trying to provide her family's basic needs and had no time or energy for anything of a spiritual nature. Nevertheless, she did miss the spiritual aspect of her life since her divorce.

Even when she and Lance had been together, he had never gone with her and the children to church. Though he'd never been a religious person, he'd been a wonderful husband and father until his affair with Leeza. Once she'd learned of his deceit, she had asked herself a million times what had ever attracted her to him. Then she would remember the man he used to be. Kind, caring and unselfish. How could she have not fallen in love with him? He'd been her dream come true.

As if seeing him and Leeza together at Brandon's games wasn't hard enough, there were the moments Hope would catch a glimpse of Leeza sitting in the front passenger seat of the car—the spot where she used to sit—when Lance came to get the kids or brought them back home. Every time she saw Leeza, she felt like jacking her up, just as she'd done when she'd first found out about the affair. Lance had tried to pull Hope off her. Then a neighbor had to get her off Lance when she'd turned on him. It was so hard now to believe that she and Leeza had ever been best friends.

Hope didn't like hating anyone. She recalled what the Bible said about loving your enemies and praying for them. She had tried often to do that concerning her ex and his new wife, but the pain and anger welling up inside of her wouldn't let her.

Hope could hear the birds singing outside her window. She couldn't remember the last time she'd done something just for herself. The rare moments when she did have a little time, she found herself too pooped to do anything but sleep.

She suddenly got the idea to treat herself to her favorite dessert, a banana split. Maybe she'd even sit in the park and eat it. An hour and a half later, she was headed out the door of her apartment.

Chapter 7

The sun sparkled on the lake like glowing crystals.

Tyla bit off a huge chunk of a fried peach pie her mother had made and licked her fingers. When she noticed Jon smiling at her, she said, "What?"

"I'm still trying to figure out where you put it."

"Put what?"

"All that food."

Tyla popped Jon on his arm. She teased, "Now that we're dating, you better watch what you say to me. Those are breaking-up words. When I was in high school, I heard that this guy told his girlfriend, who was a little on the heavy side, that he never thought he'd date a big girl. But he couldn't just leave it at that. He had the nerve to tell her he liked his women stout. And guess what she did?"

Jon chuckled and hung his head. "Sat on him?"

Tyla let out a snicker and popped his arm again. "No. She broke up with him."

"You mean she broke up with him just because he said that? Sounds like a compliment to me."

Tyla leaned back and gave Jon an evil eye. "You would say that." She rolled her eyes and mumbled, "Men."

"I like your size. You're not too big, not too little. Just the right size."

"Ah! Too late. Don't be trying to fix what you said," Tyla teased.

Jon laughed again. "Let's change the subject before I get in hot water."

Tyla took another bite of her pie. "You mean *deeper* hot water 'cause you are already there. Honey, you are sizzling. You're at the boiling point."

Jon snickered and attempted to change the subject. "So tell me more about this modeling assignment you have tomorrow."

Tyla replied through chews, "Oh, it's just me and a few other women modeling hats at one of the boutiques at the mall."

"Mind if I come?"

Tyla grabbed another tenderloin biscuit and stared at Jon. "You mean you'd really want to spend your Sunday afternoon watching me wear hats?" She took a bite of the biscuit.

"Yeah. Is a guy watching his girl modeling not cool or something?"

"No, it's not that. I just didn't think you'd be interested."

Jon looked longingly into Tyla's eyes. "If it's important to you, it's important to me."

This tender side of him was causing her to feel the butterflies again. She wanted to kiss him. They'd been dating a week and hadn't shared their first kiss yet. She wondered what it would feel like to have his lips touch hers and felt herself staring into space.

"Are you okay?" Jon asked.

Tyla covered her mouth with her hand and let out a giggle. "I'm fine."

Jon shot her a questioning gaze. "What's so funny?"

Embarrassed, Tyla simply said, "Nothing."

Tyla entered the dressing room of the boutique and blended in amongst the three other women, one Asian beauty and two attractive Caucasians.

She eyed her name on the tags pinned to the different styles of clothing hanging on the rack with matching hats. She was hoping to be among those who didn't have to change clothes except for the hats, but the store's owner and staff loved her quick changes and cool presentations. They said she knew how to make the customers want anything she wore.

As she made her way to her dressing chair and table, Tyla admired the huge array of brightly-colored hats—wide and medium brimmed, pillbox, feathered, netted, organza, and felt—a hat wearer's paradise in almost every color imaginable. Not one like the other but each chosen to fit every taste known to womankind.

Tyla took her seat and stared back at her reflection in the oval-shaped mirror. Then she touched up her hair, which she had pulled back in a plaited bun. Next, she began applying a little makeup to her cheeks, being careful not to get too close to her hairline with the foundation in order to avoid getting any on the brims of the hats she'd be wearing. She applied a small amount of color to her eyes.

Tyla stood, treaded over to the clothing rack and removed a white skirt, a white tank top, and a bright orange jacquard jacket. Most of the outfits she wore during her assignments were a little outlandish for her taste, but she liked this one.

She stepped behind the black-and-gold screen and hung the items on the metal hooks on the wall. She slipped off her tennis shoes and socks before sliding off her blue jeans. She threw the jeans over the screen and pulled on the fully-lined skirt. Then she took off her white Nike T-shirt, tossed it over the screen and carefully pulled the sleeveless top over her head. Next, she put on the jacket.

Tyla stepped from behind the screen and slipped her bare feet into a pair of orange mules before grabbing an orange wide-brimmed hat with an organza ribbon. She sashayed back to the dressing table, sat down and placed the hat on her head. She humbly admired her reflection in the mirror.

She and the other ladies complimented each other before making their grand entrances to applause from the crowd. Tyla felt the adrenaline coursing through her body as she went back and forth between the dressing room and the boutique. When the show was over, she felt a sense of fulfillment.

Jon's eyes beamed with pride as Tyla made her way over to him after the show. She stood on tiptoes to peck his left cheek. He placed his arm around her waist and gave her a gentle squeeze. "You were awesome! You looked great wearing those hats." He added, "And the outfits, too."

Tyla was glowing. She loved modeling, but it felt good to be back in her jeans, T-shirt and tennis shoes. She liked dressing up, but she was much more comfortable in her casual clothes.

"Thank you. You ready to go?"

"Yeah," Jon answered. He removed his arm from her waist and took her hand in his as they walked away.

Tyla said, "Let's stop at the food court. I'm hungry."

Jon grinned slyly.

Tyla gave him a playful punch in his side. "What? I haven't eaten since breakfast."

"I didn't say anything."

"I can tell by that grin on your face what you're thinking." She began pulling him toward one of the restaurants. "Let's get Thai." Looking up at him, she asked, "Is that okay?"

"Sure."

After ordering their food, they walked through the some-what crowded food court and found a table near the center.

Tyla's look was tender. "Will you say the blessing?"

Jon returned her gaze. "Sure."

They clasped each other's hands and bowed their heads.

"Heavenly Father, we thank you for this day and for your bringing us together in the way that you have. We thank you for this food. Please continue to watch over us and guide us in the way You would have us go. Forgive us, please, for our errors and help us to be forgiving of others. It's in Jesus's name we offer this prayer. Amen."

Tyla whispered, "Amen."

They opened their eyes and let go of each other's hands.

Tyla smiled and said, "Thank you. That was sweet."

Jon returned her smile. His eyes were laced with warmth. "I really admire you."

"Why?" Tyla asked before placing a forkful of the savory chicken dish into her mouth.

"You've got so much spunk. You know what you want, and you go for it. You go to school. You're working at the hospital, and you've got your modeling."

Tyla blushed. "Well, some people would probably call what I do dabbling."

"Dabbling is continuously jumping from one thing to another, not sure of what it is you really want to do, just scratching the surface. You're not like that. You have many talents and abilities and you're putting them to good use. I think it's good to have a variety of things you can do. You never know when you'll have to fall back on one of them."

Tyla had never thought about her situation like that. "I guess you're right. You're talented, too. To help people live a normal life again with prosthetics is so wonderful. But I also remember how much you used to love drawing. Do you still do it?"

"A little." Jon bit off a piece of spring roll.

"That's great. Draw something for me. Here," Tyla said,

sliding one of her paper napkins across the table toward him. "Do it on this."

Jon gave her a crooked smile. "Are you serious?"

"Yeah. Go ahead. Do it."

Jon placed his fork on his plate and wiped his mouth and hands. He looked at Tyla. "Got a pen?"

Tyla happily reached down into her imitation Gucci bag, pulled out a black pen and handed it to Jon.

Jon took the pen in his left hand and began his drawing.

Tyla loved watching left-handed people at work. There was something fascinating about the way they held their hand. She tried to steal a peek across the table, but Jon warned her not to look.

In a matter of minutes, he gave Tyla her pen back along with his drawing. Her eyes fell. Taken aback, she looked at him.

"This is me. I didn't know you could draw like this. How'd you do it? The only time you looked at me was to tell me not to peek and you've got everything to a T, from my hair to my clothes. That's amazing."

"Not really." Jon's tone was serious. "When you love someone like I love you, with just one glance, you remember everything about them. It's embedded, not just in your memory, but in your heart." He touched his hand to his chest.

Tyla's heart was fluttering again. "You are so sweet. You know, I feel the same way about you."

"That's good to know."

They finished eating and walked hand in hand through

the mall, talking and window-shopping. They made it out of the mall about fifteen minutes before the stores started closing at six. They talked some more on the drive to Tyla's house. The next thing Jon knew, Tyla had fallen asleep. He admired her beautiful face, which was turned sideways a little toward him, her head laying on the headrest. A soft snoring escaped her lips.

Jon's heart felt light as a feather. He still couldn't believe that he and Tyla were a couple. To fall in love with someone as special as her was truly a dream come true.

Tyla stirred a little as Jon maneuvered his champagne-colored Lexus into her mother's driveway. She opened her eyes and suddenly realized she was home. Her head still lying back on the headrest, she gazed sleepily at the love of her life.

Sitting up straight, she said, "Oh, Jon, I'm sorry. I didn't mean to fall asleep on you. Why didn't you wake me?" She began rubbing the corners of her eyes with her fingertips.

Jon grinned. "It's okay. You were resting so peacefully. I didn't want to disturb you." He playfully yet tenderly added, "Did you know you snore?"

Tyla laughed as she jerked forward a little. "No, I don't."

He nodded. "Yes, you do."

Tyla suddenly looked embarrassed.

Jon gazed at her adoringly. "Relax. You have a cute snore. It didn't sound like you were calling hogs or anything. It was nice watching you sleep." He shut off the car's engine.

Tyla blushed.

Jon shocked her when he added, "To have you by my side every day, every night, to fall asleep with you and hold you in my arms all night long, would make me even happier than I am right now."

Tyla didn't know how to respond. Her heart began to pound profusely. Was he about to ask her to make a lifelong commitment to him?

Jon turned toward her and touched her right cheek with his left hand. She gazed back at him adoringly. Never before had she seen him look so serious.

"Tyla, I love you and I want to spend the rest of my life with you. Will you marry me?"

At first, she was unable to speak. Was this real? She could think of no other person she'd rather spend the remainder of her life with. "Yes, I'll marry you."

Suddenly, Jon was out of the car and on Tyla's side with her door open. He held out his hand to her. As soon as she took his hand and was out of the car, he grabbed her into his arms and hugged her tight.

Jon took Tyla by her hand and urged her, "Come on. Let's go tell your momma." He was almost dragging her behind him.

Tyla giggled. "Okay. I'm coming."

As soon as they were inside, Myah came rushing from the kitchen, drying her hands on a dish towel. "Hey. How'd it go?" she asked, referring to her modeling assignment at the boutique. "I feel so bad that none of us were there this time."

"It's okay, Momma," Tyla assured her mother. "Jon was with me." She looked at Jon and grinned. "It went really well."

Jon concurred, "Yeah, Mrs. J. She was awesome."

Myah smiled before kissing her daughter's cheek. "She always is."

Taking her mother by the hand, Tyla said, "Momma, Jon and I have something to tell you." Leading Myah over to the living room sofa, Tyla added, "Come and sit down."

Myah obeyed. Her heart was beating excitedly. She had a feeling what their news was. She sat on the sofa between Tyla and Jon and looked from one to the other.

Jon spoke. "Mrs. J, I've asked Tyla to marry me. We're engaged."

Myah jumped up. Tyla and Jon followed suit.

"That's wonderful!" Myah exclaimed. She hugged her daughter, then Jon. "Congratulations! I'm so excited. Have you told any of the others yet?"

Tyla shook her head rapidly. "No, he just proposed a minute ago in the driveway."

Myah said, "Oh, I can't wait to tell your brothers." As an afterthought, she added, "Unless you want to tell them yourselves."

Tyla grinned. "I don't care if you tell them." Looking at Jon, she asked, "Do you mind?"

They stood in a small circle, holding hands.

Jon shook his head. "No, I don't care."

Myah asked, "Have you set a date?"

Tyla and Jon looked at each other, their eyes wide. "No," they answered.

Myah kissed both of their cheeks before departing for her bedroom.

"She's really excited," Tyla said.

Jon said, "Me, too." He led Tyla back to the sofa and pulled her down to sit beside him. "So do you want a short engagement or a long one?"

Tyla's head was in a whirl. When she'd gotten up this morning, contemplating the day, she never imagined that she and Jon would be discussing getting married.

"I don't know. Going to school part-time, it's going to take me two years to finish. Then I'll have to pass the license exam. All I have now in the way of a job is my part-time one at the hospital and my modeling. I want to finish school, but I don't want to wait two years for us to get married."

Jon urged her, "Then finish. I support you one hundred percent. You can even quit your job at the hospital and just do your modeling, if that's what you want. I make enough money to take care of both of us."

If she had been given the option of quitting her job at the hospital sooner, she probably would have jumped at the opportunity, but now she was determined to persevere and even postponed requesting a transfer. "No, I want to stay at the hospital *and* do my modeling."

"Okay. Whatever you want. I just want you to be happy."

With huge eyes full of uncertainty, Tyla looked at Jon. "So when do you want to get married?"

"Six months?"

Tyla spoke in almost a whisper. "Six months." She counted aloud on her fingers. "June, July, August, September, October, November. Today's the twenty-first. Com'ere." Jumping up, she pulled Jon along with her into the kitchen to the wall that contained the calendar. She flipped to November. "Can't do it too close to Thanksgiving because most of our family and friends will probably be out of town or visiting their families for the holiday." She frowned and looked at Jon. "It may be cold. I've kind of always wanted my wedding in the spring, but that would be another four months and I don't want to wait that long. Do you?"

"No, not really."

Placing her right index finger on a spot on the calendar, Tyla asked, "What about Saturday, November 4th?"

Jon smiled. "Sounds good to me. There's just one other thing though."

"What?" Tyla watched him stick his hand in his left pants pocket and pull out a royal-blue felt ring box. Her heart began to pound.

Jon opened the box and removed the silver half-carat wide-band princess-cut solitaire engagement ring. "I was so nervous when I proposed that I forgot this."

Tyla's heart did a tap dance as he took her left hand and slid the ring onto her finger. Huge tears welled up in her eyes.

"Jon, it's beautiful."

"Just like you," he whispered.

They shared their first kiss and it was just as Tyla imagined it would be. The butterflies in her stomach were flapping their wings like crazy.

Chapter 8

Hope rushed through the sliding glass doors, maneuvering her way to her workstation. She had put in twelve hours at the Junction yesterday, her own four-hour shift plus eight hours for a full-time coworker who had called in sick. If she hadn't needed the extra money so badly, she wouldn't have agreed to work the overtime. She was exhausted and wasn't in the mood for any of Tyla's chitchat today and hoped she'd be able to keep her distance.

As soon as the thought flashed through her mind, Hope heard an irritatingly cheery voice say, "Good morning, Hope. How you doing?"

Hope dropped her carryall and purse onto her desk. "Mornin'," she mumbled.

Tyla scooted her chair back, peered into Hope's work area, and asked, "Did you enjoy your weekend?"

Hope was leaning over. She pulled open her lower left

desk drawer, dropped in her pocketbook and carryall, and closed the drawer. She straightened, sat down and scooted her chair up to her desk. "Yes." She suddenly noticed that Tyla was standing beside her. Hope felt like ignoring her but wanted to log on to her computer. Since passwords were confidential, she didn't want anyone standing over her shoulder while she typed hers. She glared up at Tyla. "Did you need something?"

Tyla had a big, goofy grin on her face. The next thing Hope knew, Tyla had stuck her left hand, palm down, all up in her face.

Tyla explained excitedly, "I got engaged yesterday."

Hope gave the ring a quick glance and quickly murmured, "Congratulations," before turning her attention back to her computer.

Hurt and disappointed at her coworker's callous response to her good news, Tyla sadly returned to her seat. How could anybody be so cold and apprehensive toward another human being? Would it kill Hope to show some positive emotions sometimes? The woman never smiled. If she ever did, her face would probably break from the shock of it. Tyla suddenly felt bad for thinking so negatively of Hope.

As Hope logged on to her computer, she thought that if Tyla knew what was good for her, she'd stay single and not have anything to do with men, period. None of them were any good, especially once they married you. They were sweet to you while you were dating them, but after marriage, they turned into the jerks they really were.

Later that evening when Tristen met Tyla and Jon to go

horseback riding, Tristen congratulated the couple on their engagement. It was obvious to Jon that his friend was truly happy that he and Tyla were engaged. Tyla told them about Hope's reaction to the news at work that morning.

As their horses trotted beside each other, Jon reminded her, "Baby, I told you, you're trying too hard. Just leave her alone."

Tyla said, with an edge of irritation, "Jon, we have to work together. I can't just leave her alone."

Jon had never seen Tyla so uptight before. Why was she so determined to be this woman's friend when it was obvious that the lady didn't want it?

Tristen tried to reiterate what Jon had said. "Just talk to her when your job calls for communication and then leave her alone if she doesn't want to be bothered. She may warm up to you eventually."

Tyla gave her brother a sad look. "I just don't understand her." She let out a helpless sigh.

Jon offered, "What if I take you out to eat when we finish our ride? Will that make you feel better?"

"No," Tyla quickly responded.

Tristen chuckled and, looking at Jon, mumbled, "That's a first."

Tyla kept her eyes in front of her as she responded, "I heard you. Why do y'all think you can pacify me with food?"

Tristen laughed again. "'Cause it usually works."

Tyla gave her brother a fake smile.

As Tristen maneuvered his horse up ahead of Tyla and Jon, he was leaning forward bubbling over with laughter.

Tyla said to Jon, "Look at him with his ole bighead self. I

oughta catch up with him and pop him upside that big head."

Jon's mouth lifted in a huge grin.

They rode the horses back to the stable. Tyla was quiet as Jon drove them back to Myah's. When Jon heard what Myah had cooked for supper, he changed his mind about going out to eat. He had always loved Myah's fine home-cooked meals. His own mother was more of a gourmet cook, which was okay, but he preferred good old-fashioned home-cooked food.

Myah visited with her two children and future son-in-law for a few minutes before departing for her room. A few minutes later, Tristen decided it was time for him to leave. Tyla and Jon strolled into the kitchen.

Tyla sat down at the table, saying, "Well, you know where everything is. So make yourself at home and get whatever you want."

Jon said, "You mean you're not gon' fix my plate?"

Tyla drew in her head and rolled her eyes. "Something wrong with your hands?"

Jon chuckled as he got a plate and silverware. He went to the stove and began putting some food on the dish. "What about when we get married?" he joked. "Are you gonna fix my plate for me then?"

Tyla teased, "Only if you got two broke legs and can't walk, hop or crawl to the kitchen."

Jon burst out in laughter. "That's cold."

Tyla placed her elbow on the table and propped her face against her hand. "Well, you asked." Then she laughed and added, "You know I'm playing, don't you?"

"I hope so." He placed his food on the table and went over to one of the cabinets and retrieved a glass goblet. After pouring himself some sweet iced tea, he sat down. "'Cuse me," he said, before bowing his head.

Tyla kept quiet until he was done saying his blessing.

Then she tenderly expressed, "I'll love you and take care of you when you're sick and even when you're not."

Jon answered without hesitation, "I believe you." He leaned toward her and pecked her right cheek.

Tyla asked, "What do you think our marriage will be like? I mean, we've been friends for so long. You don't think we'll stop being friends once we're married, do you? You know, I've heard that happens to some people, especially after they've been married a while. Momma and Daddy never stopped being friends. I hope we'll be like that."

Jon stated emphatically, "Our marriage will be whatever we make it. That's what any marriage is—good or bad. My parents are still close, too. I'm not saying they never have any problems, but they're still together."

Tyla held her head sideways. "Some people have been married practically their entire life. Can you imagine getting married when you're thirteen, fourteen or fifteen? Not having had a chance to really enjoy life and being single."

Jon nodded. "It's hard to imagine. My dad's mom got married when she was thirteen. She's seventy-seven now. When Grandpa died, she said she was gonna stay single and enjoy what was left of her freedom."

Tyla and Jon laughed.

Tyla said, "I don't blame her. Go, Grandma!"

She eyed Jon's food, which was looking and smelling delicious. She watched him cut through his corn bread several times with his spoon, mixing chunks of it with the pinto beans on his plate. He put a spoonful of the mixture into his mouth and bit off a piece of his sliced onion. She liked the sound of the crunch the onion made when he bit into it. She loved raw onions, but she couldn't stand to be around her own self after eating them. Watching Jon eat had given her back her appetite.

Tyla fanned her hand in front of her face and said teasingly, "Woo-wee. I know somebody who won't be getting any more sugar tonight."

Jon released a light chuckle.

Then she asked, "Can I have some?"

Jon eyed her. "Some what?"

"Some of your food."

"You wouldn't fix my plate and now you're asking for my food. No, get your own."

She'd get her own eventually, but right now, she couldn't wait to get a taste. "I want some of yours." She eyed him pitifully before he raised a spoonful of his food toward her mouth.

Tyla asked, "You're not gonna trick me and pull it back when I open my mouth, are you?"

Jon grinned. "Well, I guess you're just gonna have to trust me and take your chances, aren't you?" He continued holding the spoon out to Tyla. When she still would not accept it, he started to bring it toward his own mouth, saying, "Well, if you're not going to eat it, I will."

Tyla immediately said, "No, no. Let me have it."

Jon offered her the food again and after a few brief seconds, she opened her mouth.

"Mmm, that's good. Thank you," she commented in between chews.

"You're welcome."

Tyla leaned toward Jon. He met her halfway and they shared a kiss. She savored the sweetness of his mouth on hers, onion breath and all.

The week hadn't gone by fast enough, Hope thought, barely paying attention to the film that was winding down in front of her. She hated being away from her children so much during the week. The girls weren't with their father this weekend and she loved being able to spend time with them like this. She also relished having some time away from the hospital and especially from Tyla.

Tyla's cheerful mood irritated Hope to no end. How in the world could anybody be that happy all the time? Whenever Hope would pose the question to herself, she always thought about a young woman who used to be just like Tyla, a woman full of hope and compassion. As much as Hope hated to admit it, Tyla was just like she had been at that age and even into her later years. But Hope had lost her joy. She missed the person she used to be.

As they followed the other moviegoers toward the exit sign, Brittney exclaimed, "That sure was a good movie."

Hope and Ashlee agreed wholeheartedly as they all walked down the long corridor that led back to the concession and mall area.

Hope was glad to have a Saturday afternoon to spend with her daughters. Ashlee and Brittney didn't care for camping and hadn't wanted to go with Brandon and their father.

They headed to the girls' favorite store in the mall to do some shopping with the little bit of spending money Lance had given them last night when he'd picked up Brandon.

Even though she desired to be self-sufficient, Hope didn't want Lance thinking that giving the kids a few dollars here and there was going to make up for missing child-support payments and she hadn't wasted any time last night letting him know it, either. As expensive as everything was nowadays, the girls would probably have enough money to buy only one little cheap item apiece. Hope wished she had some extra cash to give them, but after the movie, popcorn and drinks, she couldn't afford it.

The girls made their purchases and they proceeded out the store. Hope thought she heard someone behind them call out her name. She turned slightly to look back but continued walking as she did so. When she heard her name again, she told Ashlee and Brittney to wait a moment. When she turned around again, to her surprise and disappointment, she saw Tyla smiling and waving as she quickened her pace toward them. There was a young woman with her who looked to be about the same age as Tyla.

Regrettably, Hope stepped to the side out of the way of mall traffic as Tyla and her companion met up with them. Tyla was grinning, *as usual*.

Tyla and the woman stopped.

"Hey, Hope," Tyla said. "I thought that was you. What a coincidence."

Hope plastered a fake grin on her oval-shaped face. "Yeah. Hey."

Tyla looked at the two attractive young teenagers standing beside Hope and her smile grew wider. "Are these your daughters?"

"Yes," Hope answered. Looking at her girls, she nodded her head at each one as she said, "This is Ashlee and this is Brittney. Girls, this is Miss Tyla." Even though she wasn't crazy about Tyla, she wanted her girls to be respectful of her. With a bit of reluctance, she added, "We work together at the hospital."

Ashlee and Brittney smiled and said hello.

Tyla said, "Hi." She appreciated the respectful way that Hope had introduced her to her children. However, she leaned in a little toward them and said, "Just call me Tyla." Looking at Hope, she added, "If that's okay with your mom." Turning her attention back to the teenagers, she said, "*Miss* makes me feel old." She made a face, humped up her shoulders and shook her head.

The teenagers giggled.

As soon as the word *old* was out of her mouth, Tyla considered that she'd probably just offended Hope with her remark. She prayed that Hope hadn't taken offense to her comment.

Tyla stepped back, placing a gentle hand on her companion's shoulder, and added, "This is my friend Olivia. She's also my youngest brother's girlfriend."

Olivia smiled. "Hi."

"Hello," the teenagers responded.

Hope and Olivia looked at one another and gave each other a friendly greeting.

Tyla asked the teenagers, "Are y'all enjoying a day out with your mom?"

The girls grinned and said, "Yes."

Brittney added, "We saw a movie."

Tyla exclaimed, "Was it good?"

Brittney and Ashlee's excitement showed on their faces as they nodded their heads.

"Yes. We liked it," Ashlee said.

A satisfied look filled Tyla's eyes. "That's great."

Hope decided to cut short the chitchat. If left up to Tyla, they'd be here all day talking. "Well, girls, we gotta go."

Tyla said, "It was nice meeting you, Ashlee, Brittney."

Ashlee said, "It was nice to meet you, too."

"'Bye," the girls said.

Tyla and Olivia echoed, "'Bye."

Hope started to walk away with her daughters tagging along beside her.

As Tyla and Olivia made their way toward the escalator, Olivia said, "So that's your coworker you've been telling us about—the one who's so mean to you?"

They stepped onto the escalator and held on to the rail as they went toward the top level.

"She's not mean," Tyla whispered, looking over her shoulder at Olivia. "She's just different than anybody I've ever known."

"I wish I could be like you."

Tyla looked back over her shoulder again. "What are you talking about?"

"You're so persistent."

"What d'you mean by that?"

"You keep going out of your way to be nice to her and she keeps knocking you down. If somebody did me like that, I wouldn't waste any more of my time trying to be their friend. Your feelings sure aren't easy to get hurt."

"I have feelings."

"I didn't say you don't *have* feelings. I said they're not easy to get hurt. If they are, you sure don't show it."

They stepped off the escalator and moved steadily through the crowd toward the mall's exit.

"That lady back there—" Olivia nodded back toward the mall "—she doesn't know what she's missing by continuously rejecting you."

Tyla had her hand on the car's door handle. "That's a really sweet thing for you to say, Olivia. I appreciate it." She opened the door and pressed the unlock button for the other doors.

"Well, I mean it," Olivia said as she climbed inside the car.

Although Tyla truly appreciated what Olivia had told her, she didn't see anything special about herself. She didn't know any other way to be.

but then she'd remember that no matter what he'd done, he was still their father and they needed him.

Lance exclaimed, "Hey, you two! How was your weekend? I bet you wish you'd come camping with me and Brandon. We had a good time."

Brittney uttered, "And be out in the woods with bears, snakes and all kinds of crawling creatures? I don't think so."

Lance pulled his youngest daughter a little closer. "Ah, girl. I need to toughen you up." He glanced at Ashlee, drawing her closer as well. "Your sister, too. Y'all just used to being around your mama. You need to hang out with me a little more."

Hope felt like telling him that if he hadn't cheated on her, he'd have more time to spend with his children.

The humor faded from Lance's eyes. "I need to talk to your mama for a minute."

Ashlee and Brittney said goodbye and went to their room.

Begrudgingly, Hope stepped outside with him. She looked toward his car, a nice older-model powder-blue Cadillac. She half expected to see Leeza sitting in it but didn't, which pleased her. The less she had to see the two of them together, the better. The mental pictures of them with each other during their affair were bad enough. Constantly thinking about what they had done to her and the fact that they were now a married couple didn't help the situation. Actually seeing them with each other always made her pain and resentment rise.

Hope folded her arms in front of her. "What's wrong with Brandon? He was fine when he left here with you Friday night."

Chapter 9

As soon as Brandon walked into the apartment, Hope could tell from the scowl on his face that something had put him in a foul mood.

"Hey. Did you enjoy your camping trip?"

"Yeah," her son answered as he brushed past her, his overnight bag thrown over his right shoulder.

She was about to ask what was wrong when she noticed Lance standing in the doorway. "What's wrong with Brandon?" she asked. She made her way toward the door.

"Can we talk outside a minute?" her ex-husband requested.

Before Hope could answer, Ashlee and Brittney came running toward their father, each throwing their arm around him. It was obvious that they loved the knucklehead. A part of her hated that they did. Sometimes she found herself wanting them to hate him as much as she did,

Lance said, "He's mad because I brought him home."

Hope hissed, "What d'you mean he's mad because you brought him home? He lives here, doesn't he? Where else you gonna take him?"

Lance responded with some reluctance. "He wants to live with me and Leeza. He—"

Hope's mouth fell open. "What?"

Lance reconsidered mentioning Leeza's name again. "He wants to live with me. We were thinking maybe you could let him stay with us for a while."

If looks could kill, Lance had no doubt that the one his ex-wife was giving him at the moment would have him six feet under.

Hope dropped her head and shook it a few times before looking back up at him. "Are you crazy? Brandon is *my* son and he's staying with me."

Lance gave her a pitiful look. "Hope, that's not fair. He's my son, too. He wants to stay with me. Can't you let him? For a few months, at least?"

Hope threw her hands in the air and screamed, "That's not fair? Oh, I feel so sorry for you." Tapping her index finger in his chest two times, she seethed as she said, "*You* slept with my best friend and broke up our family. You've got a lot of nerve. I'll tell you what's not fair."

She began poking her index finger in his chest again as he started backing away. "*You* and my best friend sleeping together. And now you've got the gall to try and take my son away from me. *You* were the one who messed up. Don't be trying to use him as an excuse to get what you want. You made your bed. Now lie in it." She turned on her heel and started to walk away.

"Hope." Lance reached out and grabbed her arm.

She snatched herself from his hold. "Let go of me."

Lance called out to her. "It's not like that. He wants me and him to have more time together. I'm his father. He needs me just as much as he does you."

Hope turned around abruptly. She was mean when she was mad. Lance had never seen this side of her until his affair with Leeza. He knew he'd brought out the worst in her with what he'd done, but he couldn't change the past. As hard as it was, they all had to get on with their lives. The scowl on her face now had him thinking he should run for cover, but he wasn't backing down from her this time, no matter how angry she was.

Hope responded mockingly, "Oh, now you finally see that you're his father and he needs you. Too bad you didn't think of that sooner. You're already behind in your child-support payments. I bust my behind day in and day out trying to take care of our children while you only have yourself and your precious Leeza to worry about. If you want to continue seeing any of them, you better get off your rump and catch up your payments. Don't say anything else to me about Brandon living with you 'cause it's not gonna happen. You may as well leave because I don't have anything else to say to you."

Hope went back inside her apartment and slammed the door shut.

Ashlee and Brittney were now in the living room.

Ashlee asked, "Mama, what's wrong?"

Hope didn't respond but went straight to Brandon's bedroom door and knocked hard several times.

"Brandon, open this door!" she yelled. "I'm not playing. If you know what's good for you, you'll open this door right now. I mean it!"

When the door opened, Hope went in and closed it behind her. Brandon made his way back to the rickety metal drawing table that also served as his desk. He sat down.

Hope wanted to tread lightly for she knew that the divorce had probably affected Brandon emotionally in ways she was yet to comprehend. She walked slowly toward him. "Your dad says you want to live with him. Is that true?"

Without looking up, the teenager mumbled, "Yeah."

Hope snapped before she could stop herself. "It's not *yeah*. It's *yes, ma'am*. Try again."

"Yes, ma'am," he uttered.

"Why? Are you unhappy here with me and your sisters?"

"No. I just wanna live with Dad. I miss him and I wanna be with him."

Hope's tone became somewhat mellow. "Brandon, honey, I understand that you miss your dad. So do Ashlee and Brittney. Whatever problems he and I have, he's still your father and I want you to see him and spend time with him. That's why I agreed to let y'all spend the weekends and some holidays with him. But I won't agree to you moving in with him. I want you here with me and Ashlee and Brittney."

This time, Brandon looked at his mother, his eyes wet

with unshed tears. "But I wanna live with Dad. Doesn't it matter what I want?"

"Yes, it does, but you're sixteen years old. You're still a minor in the eyes of the law, which makes me responsible for you. I'm your parent so I decide where you live."

Brandon didn't bat an eye or stumble over one word when he calmly stated, "I could just run away, you know, and go to Dad's anyway if I wanted to."

Hope couldn't believe her ears. She felt like grabbing him and trying to shake some sense into him, but instead she said, "I don't think you want to do that."

"Why not? He's my father. If I run away to his house, the court'll let me stay with him."

"No, they won't because I'm your legal guardian and I say you live here."

When Brandon didn't respond, Hope said, "Listen. You, Brittney, Ashlee and I have always been close. When your father was here, we were close to him, too. You can still be with your dad but not the way you want to. I don't want this to cause any more friction between us than it already has. I'm trying hard to take care of us. As the oldest, I need your support. I love you very much, Brandon. I know you think I'm hard on you at times, but it's only because I love you and want the best for you. Do you understand what I'm saying?"

Brandon answered in a quiet tone. "Yes."

Hope moved in closer, leaned down and kissed the top of her son's head. "We'll talk some more later, if you want to." Then she left the room.

Brandon thought back to the time when they were all one big, happy family. Not being able to be with his father every day was a real kick in the pants. He wanted more. Needed more.

Only two more days of school left. Hope glanced at her bedside clock the next morning, not at all eager to get up. Had she been too hard on Brandon last night? She supposed she could let him and the girls spend at least a month of their summer vacation with their father, but the thought of her children being away from her for an entire month sent chills down her spine.

The weeks that they spent away at basketball and band camps were hard enough. As soon as Brandon returned home from his, it seemed that it was time for the girls to leave for theirs. Hope always had terrible withdrawal symptoms whenever they were away from her.

A banging on her bedroom door brought Hope out of her musings. She sat up in bed. "Come in."

In burst Ashlee and Brittney.

Startled, Hope asked, "What is it?"

Brittney was out of breath when she spoke. "Brandon's gone." She stopped to catch her breath.

Ashlee finished. "He's not here. We looked everywhere."

Hope threw back the covers and jumped from the bed. "What d'you mean he's not here?"

The girls followed their mother out into the hallway.

Brittney said, "He's gone. He must've run away."

They trailed behind Hope into Brandon's room. The

covers were pulled back on his bed, and his closet door was open. Hope dashed from the room with Ashlee and Brittney still in her tracks and went to every room in the apartment, searching for Brandon and calling out his name.

Hope threw her hands to her mouth. "Oh, Lord, where can he be?"

She grabbed the phone from the receiver and quickly dialed Lance. As soon as he answered the phone, she frantically asked, "Is Brandon there?"

Confused, Lance said, "What?"

"Brandon. Is he there?"

"No. What's going on?"

Hope quickly explained, "We've looked everywhere. He's not here in the apartment. We don't know where he is."

Lance instructed, "Call 911. I'll be right there."

As soon as the call to Lance had ended, Hope dialed 911 and informed them that her sixteen-year-old son was missing.

Two officers, one male and one female, were writing up the police report when Lance arrived. Hope gave them a recent school photo of Brandon to enter into their database. After the officers had gone, Hope instructed Ashlee and Brittney to hurry and get ready for school before their bus came.

Brittney complained, "Mama, we can't go to school not knowing where Brandon is or if he's all right. Can't we stay home?"

"No," Hope answered. "You've only got two more days of school. As soon as I find out where he is, I'll call the school and let you know."

Finally, the girls were ready for school and bid their parents goodbye before going to catch their bus.

Hope stood at the living room window watching Ashlee and Brittney as they waited for their bus.

Without turning away from the window, she expressed effortlessly, "I thought everything was okay last night after he and I talked. He said something about running away, but after we talked, I didn't think anything else about it. I should've known something like this would happen."

Lance wasn't quite sure what to do or say. This was all his fault. Even if Hope didn't continuously remind him that it was, he knew that he was to blame. He wanted to reach out to her and console her, but she'd probably slap him in the face if he tried.

Hope folded one arm across her stomach and covered her face with her other hand. Her body began to tremble.

When Lance heard her crying, he walked up beside her and gently took her in his arms. The angry Hope wanted to push him away, but the sad and lonely Hope threw her arms around him, buried her face in his chest and let the tears flow.

When Hope hadn't arrived at work by eight-thirty, Tyla asked their supervisor about her and was told that she'd had a family emergency and wouldn't be in. Tyla hoped that everything was all right with Hope and her family.

Jon met Tyla for lunch in the hospital cafeteria.

"How's that training manual coming along?" he asked as he scooped up a spoonful of chicken potpie and put it in his mouth.

"Okay. I'm still learning so it's a slow process. I'm just writing it as I go and using the notes I've already taken. Maybe I'll have it finished by the time I complete my nursing studies," she added with a chuckle.

Jon chuckled lightly.

Tyla stuck her fork into a cool, crisp slice of cucumber. Her supervisor had been so impressed with the notes she'd taken during her training that she'd asked her to do a registration procedure manual for the E.R. Tyla felt honored but it was hard to write about something she couldn't fully comprehend. She added a medium-sized piece of romaine lettuce to her fork before sticking it in her mouth.

Jon asked, "How's school?"

"Fine. My anatomy and physiology class is kicking my behind, but I'm trying to hang in there."

"Don't give up. You'll make a great nurse. You're empathetic and compassionate. And you're a good listener, too."

Tyla recalled her orientation class at school where one of the instructors told the students what it would take for them to succeed. Among the list of qualities she had mentioned, the ones Jon had just named were included. It made Tyla feel good that despite her imperfections, people still saw her good qualities. That was how she tried to see others, too, which was why she had not given up on becoming a friend to Hope, even though Hope still treated her like she had the bubonic plague.

"That's sweet. Thank you. Tell me more about this project you're working on." Tyla loved hearing about Jon's job. It sounded so interesting and exciting. She took a sip of her bottled water.

Jon spoke with ease. "There are dozens of research teams around the world working on developing artificial organs such as eyes, hearts, livers and kidneys."

Tyla's eyes grew huge. "You're kidding."

Jon shook his head. "No, I'm serious. Almost any disability you can think of, there's probably research already underway to overcome it. Our team at Mercy is working with Johns Hopkins University in Baltimore on silicon retinas. A researcher there has already implanted light-sensitive chips in the eyes of fifteen patients."

"Wow," Tyla said, "that's incredible. It's amazing what can be done through modern technology. You know who it makes me think about?"

Jon looked at her, his eyes full of interest. "Who?"

Tears poked at Tyla's eyes when she answered, "Jesus. When he was on earth, God gave him the power of healing. Jesus was so compassionate, just like his father. I'm so proud of you. What you and others are doing to help people with disabilities is so commendable."

Jon stated casually, "Thank you, but I don't do it to be praised. I do it because I care."

A smile tugged at the corners of Tyla's mouth. "I know. And I hope I didn't offend you by saying that. I just think what you and others are doing is good. We're so quick to tell people when they do something we don't like. I think we should be just as quick about letting them know when they do something we do like."

Jon's smile was filled with warmth. "You're right. That's how it should be." Checking his watch, he said, "We better be going."

Tyla's heart dropped to the pit of her stomach. She was so enjoying her time and conversation with Jon that she wasn't ready for it to end. He put her dishes on his tray and placed her tray underneath his. They stood and made their way to the huge trash can near the door of the cafeteria. They chatted as they headed back toward the emergency room.

In the hallway, Jon said, "See you tonight."

Tyla said, "Okay."

He gave her left cheek a quick peck and she watched him walk away. She admired his bowlegged walk in his black dress pants. The pastel pink long-sleeved shirt he wore complemented the dark slacks.

Tyla hummed as she made her way to her desk. When she saw their coworker LaPorsha sitting at Hope's station registering a patient, she wondered again if things were okay with Hope.

Chapter 10

At the police station, Hope and Lance had tried unsuccessfully to get the police to drop the runaway charge against Brandon. The officers had found him walking in the direction of Lance's house. The arresting officer informed them that the matter had been turned over to juvenile court and gave them a court date of June fifth, the following Monday.

When Hope and Lance took Brandon to school, they had talked with the school counselor who assured them that she would make sure that Ashlee and Brittney were notified immediately that their brother had been located and was at school.

Now that Hope knew Brandon was all right, she was seething again with anger at Lance and Leeza. If it weren't for them, Brandon never would have run away. No matter how hard she tried, she couldn't stop blaming them. Listening to Lance as he drove her home talking about how well things had turned out only made her angrier.

Hope folded her arms and glared at him. "You know, this never would've happened if you hadn't been sleeping around with Leeza and broke up our family."

Lance's tone was empathetic. "You're right and you have every right to blame me. It's all my fault, but I never meant to hurt you or the kids. I can't explain how or why it happened, Hope. But it did and I don't blame you for hating me. But we've got to get past it for our children's sake, especially for Brandon."

Hope spit out, "Oh, now you're worried about our children. Why didn't you think about them when you were sleeping around? What was on your mind then besides yourself and Leeza?" She turned to stare out her window. Her tone turned soft for a brief moment. "We were happy, or so I thought." Then just as quickly, her mood turned sour. She gave him a critical glare. Her voice was layered with regret and grief. "You destroyed our family and everything we had. I'll never forgive you and Leeza for what you did. Pull over and let me out."

Lance looked at her for a brief moment. It was clear that she was angry, but was she serious? "What?"

"You heard me. Pull over and let me outta here."

"Hope, you can't be serious. Let me take you home. It's more than five miles to your apartment. You don't need to be walking the streets alone in your condition."

Hope stared at him. "Why are you acting all concerned about me now? You didn't give a flip about me when we were married. I said pull over and let me out."

Lance was beginning to see that his ex-wife's hatred of him ran far deeper than he had thought. He had destroyed their family and would probably end up paying for it for the rest of his life. He didn't know what to do. He was afraid that, considering the state Hope was in, that she might open up the door and jump out while he was still driving if he didn't stop.

He started slowing down and pulled the car over to the curb. When Hope exited the vehicle, he sat there for a few minutes. He watched her walk down the sidewalk ahead of the car. Then he gradually pulled away. When he passed her, he kept her in sight in his rearview mirror until he could see her no more.

Hope didn't know how long it had taken her to get home. Once inside the apartment, she fell across her bed and cried.

Hope and Lance were relieved that the judge had only imposed a ninety-day probationary sentence on Brandon, whereby he'd have to report to a social services aide in the juvenile probation office once a month.

As instructed, Hope called the juvenile probation office and set up the initial appointment for Brandon to report with both her and Lance. The appointment was for the next day at nine o'clock.

Hope knocked on Brandon's bedroom door and heard him answer for her to come in.

After she'd informed him of his appointment the next day, she said, "You know, I've been thinking. If you still want a part-time job, you can get one this summer while school's out, but you'll have to quit when school starts back. I think a job will take away too much time from your studies and you've already got basketball."

When Brandon looked at her, there was a slight hint of a sparkle of hope in his eyes. Hope hadn't seen it in a long time.

He said, "I don't have transportation. How am I gonna get back and forth to work?"

"I know somebody who has a car for sale. It's an old model, but in good condition."

"I thought you said we couldn't afford to buy a car."

"Don't worry about it. Your dad and I will work it out."

Brandon jumped up from his seat, smiling. His voice was raspy yet filled with joy. "I'll help pay for it, too. I know how hard you work trying to take care of us. I wanna help."

Hope put her arms around her son and for the first time in a long while, he let her and hugged her back. It felt good to have her oldest child in her arms again. Brandon was hurt and angry just as she was. She didn't think he could help venting his frustration any more than she could.

She said silently, *Lord, help me.*

The truth was she had no idea how she was going to pay for the car she'd just promised her son. She hadn't even discussed it with Lance, who probably wasn't going to help her pay for it anyway. She would find a way, though, even if it killed her.

The social services aide, a woman who appeared to be very young, had seemed nice. Hope had thought that

Brandon's caseworker would be an older person, perhaps a man. With Brandon and Lance behind her, Hope opened the door to exit the building. Just as she did so, she came close to hitting a man who was making his entrance.

"'Cuse me," she offered.

"No problem," the man said. He stepped back and held the door open for them.

Catching a quick glimpse of the woman's face as she passed by, the man was hit with the realization that he knew her from somewhere.

He was still trying to remember where he'd seen her when he entered the receptionist's area to sign back in from his home visit and check the message center to see if he had any messages.

As he was signing in, the receptionist said, "Tristen, you have some messages in your message slot. Your voice mail is full."

He grabbed his messages and said, "Thanks, Patty. I'll clean out my mailbox." As he made his way to his office, Tristen thought once more about the woman and where he'd seen her before, but nothing else came to mind.

Chapter 11

On Friday night, Jon took Tyla on a carriage ride after dinner.

Tyla exclaimed, "This is nice. I've never been on a carriage ride before."

"Really?" Jon said. "If I'd known that, I would've saved it for our wedding day."

"Why?"

Jon squeezed her hand. "I just want that day to be special for you."

"It'll still be special." Tyla leaned back. "You just take me on all the carriage rides you want to."

Jon teased, "Oh, you'd love that, wouldn't you?"

They enjoyed the remainder of their ride before exiting the carriage in the park.

Tyla said, "I could eat some ice cream. You?"

Jon glanced at his watch. "We just ate two hours ago."

"So. We didn't have dessert." Pulling him alongside her, she said, "Come on," and led him to her favorite ice cream shop.

Since it was nice outside, they chose to sit at one of the patio tables on the cobblestones.

Jon said, "Tristen told me you have another modeling assignment tomorrow. Why didn't you tell me? You know I love to see you in action."

"Well, this is different than when I'm modeling in stores and on runways. This is an actual photo shoot. A lot of agents frown on bringing people with you. Besides, I'll be wearing wedding gowns for a bridal magazine. I didn't tell you because I don't want you to see me in a wedding gown yet."

His eyes wide, Jon asked, "Are you serious?"

Tyla's eyes met his. "Yeah."

"Why not?"

"Jon, everybody knows the bride doesn't want to be seen in her wedding dress by her groom until she's walking down that aisle. If he sees her in her dress before then, it's just not the same. When you see me for the first time in my dress, I want the sight of me to take your breath away."

Jon licked a dab of strawberry ice cream from the corner of his mouth. "Well, that already happens every time I see you."

"That's really sweet, but you still can't come."

Tyla eyed him from the corner of her eye. He was busy eating his ice cream and seemed to be enjoying it.

"Are you mad?" she asked.

"No, I'm not mad." He kept his eyes glued to his dessert.

"Thanks for understanding," Tyla expressed affectionately.

Jon taunted her. "Do I have a choice? Women always get their way. Weddings are a prime example. The men don't exist until y'all want somebody tall, dark and handsome for you to walk down the aisle with. I mean, the man can be looking good and all everybody sees is the bride. He might as well be invisible. It's all about the woman. Her big day. Everybody looking at her. Her hair, her flowers, her dress."

His little pity speech amused her. She leaned sideways a little and looked him up and down before standing and discarding her empty cup into the trash. "I don't know where *that* came from. That ice cream must've given you a brain freeze. Are you ready to go or do you wanna whine some more?"

Jon stood and threw away his trash. Shaking his head, he uttered, "See. What'd I just say? I may as well have been talking to myself."

Hooking her arm in his, Tyla said, "I thought you was."

Jon let out a short laugh. "Whew! You're a handful tonight."

Hope was exhausted. She had put in a full day at the hospital and had to work three hours in the Junction's garden shop. She'd managed to get Brandon on the bus yesterday for basketball camp and couldn't wait for him to get back home on Saturday. He would start his part-time job at Wendy's on Monday. She had already picked up the car she was buying for him, a 1987 teal Chevrolet Cavalier. She could hardly wait for him to see it when he returned from camp.

Hope had just returned to her register after watering the plants in the outdoor garden section when she looked up at an older black couple, standing in front of her, dripping wet. She wondered what had happened to them. She looked outside to see if it had started raining.

Hope extended them a friendly greeting and asked, "May I help you?"

The man's eyeglasses were in his left hand and he was wiping his face with his right hand. "We wanna speak to the manager."

Hope stared at him. "Is there a problem, sir?"

Before the gentleman could speak, the woman with him glared at Hope, pointed and said, "That's her, James. She's the one who got us all wet a while ago when she was watering those plants."

Hope pressed her left hand to her chest. "Ah, I did what?"

The woman shouted, "Don't be playing dumb. You know what you did. You got us all wet out there watering those plants." She pointed toward the door to the outside garden area. "You need to pay attention to what you're doing. We wanna speak to the manager."

Hope looked regrettably from the irate woman to the man, then back to the woman. "I'm sorry. I didn't know I got you wet. It was an accident." Reaching on a shelf below her register, she pulled out a roll of paper towels. She handed them to the man since he seemed much calmer.

The woman probably would have shoved them back at her. She repeated, "I'm sorry."

The man took the towels while the woman ranted, "I told you we wanna see the manager."

James began wiping down the woman with a wad of the paper towels. "Emma, calm down. She said she's sorry."

Emma pushed his hand away. "Don't you tell me to calm down. Why you takin' up for her? A minute ago, you were mad, too."

James wiped his face and the top of his half-bald head with another wad of paper towels. "I know, but it was an honest mistake."

"How many times do I have to say I wanna talk to the manager?" Emma glared at Hope. "Are you gonna get your manager or do I have to pitch a conniption up in here?"

Lines were beginning to form at both registers and people were staring at the commotion.

James took Emma by the arm. "Emma, calm down. Let's go."

Emma snatched her arm from his grip. "If you tell me to calm down one more time, somebody's gon' have to pull me off you. I said I wanna talk to the manager."

James looked sorrowfully at Hope.

Hope gave him an understanding nod and said, "It's okay. I'll call the manager." She was about to do so when a man approached them.

He asked, "Hope, what's wrong?" Then he looked at James and Emma.

Hope answered, "When I was outside watering the plants,

I accidentally got these two customers wet. I've apologized. I didn't see them."

Emma said, "She should've been paying attention to what she was doing. We were out there minding our own business, looking at some flowers and the next thing we knew, we were soaking wet. I want her fired."

Panic ran its course through Hope. She pleaded, "Mr. Randall, please don't fire me. I need this job." Before she realized it, she was broadcasting her business out loud for all to hear. "I'm a single parent. I have three teenagers to take care of. I said I was sorry."

Suddenly, a younger-looking man appeared at the register, pushing a shopping cart, stating comically, "Do y'all have an automatic sprinkler system outside? You need to keep an eye on it if you do. I got wet while I was looking at some plants. I just took a shower before I came up here."

Emma pointed at the man and squealed. "See there! She got him wet, too. I told you I want her fired." She huffed, "Humph. Gettin' people wet."

Hope lost control of her emotions as fear of losing her job raced through her like a speeding locomotive. She looked at the man who'd just come in. "Sir, I'm sorry." Then she looked back at the manager. "Mr. Randall, I didn't see them. If I lose this job, I can't take care of my kids."

The younger man thought Hope looked familiar. When he'd walked in, he'd heard her saying something about being a single parent and having three teenagers to take care of. His heart went out to her. He didn't want her to lose her job. It wasn't a big deal to him. He'd only complained in jest as he was coming in to pay for some flowers he'd gotten for his mother.

The manager did not want to lose one of the store's best employees. He thought quickly to come up with a solution that would please the female customer. "Ma'am, Ms. Mason is one of my best employees. You have every right to be upset. Would it please you if I gave you your choice of any plant you want in the garden shop plus a fifty-dollar gift card?"

The rage in Emma's eyes was replaced with a sparkle. She tried not to reveal her delight. "I guess that'll be okay."

"All right," the manager said. "Pick out any plant you want and it's yours, free of charge." He grabbed one of the gift cards at Hope's register and handed it to Hope. "Ring this up for fifty dollars and give it to her when she comes back in."

The man and woman headed outside to pick out their plant.

The manager looked at the younger man. "Sir, what about you? Would that suit you, too?" He nodded toward the flowers in the cart. "No charge for your plants and we'll give you a fifty-dollar gift card as well?"

The man answered, "No, that won't suit me."

Both Hope and the manager were panic-stricken.

The manager asked, "Well, sir, what can we do for you?"

The young man answered, "Well, it's obvious that she's upset about this whole situation. Can you let her take a break to calm her nerves? There's a McDonald's in here, isn't there?"

Hope shot him a grateful look.

The manager answered, "Yes, there is. That's very considerate of you. Sure she can take a break. Is that all?"

"Not quite." The man turned to Hope and asked, "Do you mind if I join you?"

Hope's gratitude soon turned to fury. He looked like he was young enough to be her son. Was this little joker trying to flirt with her, and in her boss's presence? She felt like telling him to take a hike.

"Sir—"

The young man held out his hand to her and said, "Hope, my name's Tristen Jefferson. I don't mean any disrespect. I—"

Hope simply stared at him. How did he know her name? Suddenly, she remembered and looked down at her name tag pinned to the left side of her apron. His brazen attitude had scrambled her brain. "Mr. Jefferson—"

He took his hand back and smiled, showing perfect white teeth. "Tristen."

She wished he'd stop interrupting her. "Mr. Jefferson," she repeated, "I appreciate your thoughtfulness, but I'm working. I don't need a break. I'm fine." Hope looked at the manager and said, "Mr. Randall, please deduct the cost of the plants and the gift card from my check."

The manager said, "It's okay. The store will cover it."

Tristen kindly interjected, "I'll pay for my plants, and I don't want a gift card."

The man said, "Whatever you wish, Mr. Jefferson." Upon hearing his name being called over the intercom, he politely excused himself.

Hope now realized that the other customers had left her line and gone to the other register. Her heart raced as she rang up Tristen's flowers. She said nothing even though she felt his eyes on her. He was making her nervous. She couldn't ring his plants up fast enough.

When she gave him his change, she said, without looking in his face, "Thank you for shopping at the Junction. Come again."

Tristen put his change in his wallet and grabbed the two plastic bags of flowers. He sensed her anger and whispered, "I wasn't trying to come on to you, although you are a very beautiful woman. I just thought you needed a break and maybe someone to talk to."

He waited for her to respond. When she didn't, he said, "Have a good evening," and walked away.

Hope had come close to losing her job. She appreciated how the young man had come to her rescue, but she didn't care for his forward attitude and she could care less if she'd hurt his feelings. Better his than hers. He'd said he wasn't trying to come on to her, but she wasn't born yesterday. And his little compliment about her being beautiful didn't impress her, either. She'd gotten rid of one pain in the neck. She didn't need another one to take his place. Even if he weren't so young, she didn't want another man in her life. She didn't know if she ever would.

Chapter 12

Hope had felt lost with Brandon at his dad's and Ashlee and Brittney away at band camp. As soon as she saw the girls getting off the bus, she ran to greet them.

When she threw her arms around each one and kissed them on their cheeks, Ashlee wiped her face and reminded her mother, "Mama, not in public."

Hope felt a pang of hurt at her eldest daughter's protest, but quickly dismissed it. "Did you have a good time?"

Brittney exclaimed, "It was fun! We learned a lot of new routines."

Hope said, "I can't wait to see 'em. Come on. Grab your bags."

The teenagers got their luggage and walked with their mother toward the car.

Brittney asked, "Where's Brandon?"

Hope answered, "He's with your dad. He'll be home later

today. So what do you two want to do this afternoon? Are you tired?"

Ashlee answered, "Kind of."

Brittney asked, "Can we stop by the video store on the way home and rent a movie?"

Hope said, "Sure. That sounds like a good idea."

At the video store, they couldn't agree on a movie to rent.

Brittney handed her mother one that was rated PG-13. "Can we get this one?"

As usual, Hope turned the video over in her hands and read the back label. *Violence. Strong language and some sexual content.* Handing it back to her daughter, she firmly stated, "No, find something else."

Brittney protested, "Why can't we see this one?"

Hope asked, "Did you read the back? Violence, sexual content and strong language. I don't want you watching that kinda stuff."

Brittney mumbled, "Well, Daddy lets us watch 'em at his house."

Hope thought she would explode right there in the store. "He does?"

Ashlee was rolling her eyes sideways at her sister in an effort to keep her quiet.

Brittney responded, "Yeah. Him and Miss Leeza said it's okay."

Hope felt a raging storm brewing in her belly. She snatched the movie from Brittney's hand and placed it back onto the shelf. "Well, you can't see it. Find something else."

Brittney protested, "But there's nothing else good to see."

Hope waved her arms through the air. "Brittney, all these movies in here and there's nothing else good to see?"

She was about to ask the people who had turned to stare at them what they were looking at when Brittney whined, "Mama, you always want us to watch G-rated movies. We're not little kids anymore. You're too old-fashioned."

Hope spun around on her youngest daughter as though she was about to pin her up against the wall. "What did you say?"

The anger Brittney saw in her mother's eyes she had not seen except the day her mother had found out about her father's affair with Leeza. Brittney backed away like a frightened puppy.

Ashlee grabbed her sister by the hand, leading her to another section of videos. "Come on. I'll help you find something."

Hope was still seething when they got home. As soon as Brandon walked through the door, she told him to keep an eye on the girls while she ran an errand.

Hope pounded on the front door of Lance and Leeza's house.

When Leeza answered, she frantically asked, "What's wrong?"

Hope brushed past her former best friend, asking, "Where's Lance? I need to talk to him."

Leeza followed Hope. "He's not here. Didn't you see his car isn't in the garage? He went to the store."

Hope was so enraged that she guessed she must have

overlooked that little detail. She spun around and demanded, "You get his butt on his cell phone and tell him I need to talk to him right now."

Panic and fear rose in Leeza's chest. "Hope, what's wrong? Are the kids okay?"

Hope screamed, "I said I wanna talk to *him*. Brushing past Leeza again, she said, "I'll be outside in my car waiting on him." She slammed the door behind her.

About fifteen minutes later, Lance pulled into the driveway. Before he could exit his vehicle, Hope was on him, pounding her fists against his chest.

"How dare you!"

Lance attempted to get his ex-wife off him. "Hope, what's wrong? Leeza called and said you were over here pitchin' a fit. Why you actin' all crazy?"

Hope kept hitting him. "I'm trying to raise our children the best way I know how and you and your wife in there are trying to mess up everything I'm trying to do to steer them in the right direction."

Lance managed to get away from her and ran to the opposite side of his car. He stared across the hood at Hope. "What are you talkin' about?"

As Hope walked around the front of the car, Lance approached the rear. "What kinda mess have you and Leeza been letting my children watch? What kind of videos and TV programs? I was in the video store a while ago with Ashlee and Brittney. Brittney was giving me a fit about what video to get and she said you and Leeza let them watch violent videos with sex in 'em."

Hope continued to go after Lance as he tried to explain.

"Now, Hope, wait a minute. They're teenagers. You can't expect them to still watch those li'l kiddie movies they watched when they were young. The movies me and Leeza let them watch weren't all that bad."

Hope bellowed, "You dirty, rotten…"

Just then, they noticed flashing blue lights in the driveway.

Two uniformed officers, a male and a female, exited the police car.

The male officer inquired, "What seems to be the problem here?"

Lance responded, "Nothing, Officer. Everything's fine."

The officer responded, "That's sure not what it looks like."

Hope pointed to Lance, turned to the officers and said, "This jerk is putting trash in our kids' heads and I want it to stop."

The female officer asked Hope to explain. Hope told them about the incident in the video store.

The officers certainly understood Hope's concern but told her that this wasn't the way to solve the problem.

When they asked Lance if he wanted to press charges against Hope, Hope went ballistic.

She yelled, "Press charges? Why you asking *him* if he wants to press charges against *me*? *I'm* the one who should be pressing charges against *him*. Number one, for being an adulterer. Number two, for enticing our children for indecent purposes with the mess he's been letting them look at through videos and on TV."

The female officer surmised that Hope was definitely over the edge. Nevertheless, they had to take her complaint seriously. She asked, "What kind of videos and TV programs, ma'am? Pornographic?"

Hope suddenly felt defeated. In her heart, she knew that Lance would never expose their children to such viewing, but she still didn't like the fact that he was being too lenient with them regarding the types of movies they watched when they stayed with him.

She repeated part of what she'd already told them. "All I know is I took my two teenage daughters to the video store this afternoon. And my youngest, who just recently turned fourteen, started complaining when I wouldn't rent a PG-13 violent video with strong language and sexual content like the ones he—" Hope nodded at Lance "—and his wife let them watch. I'm trying to raise my children to have morals and I don't need him and his wife interfering with that."

The female officer politely responded, "That's very commendable. There should be more parents like you, but unless your husband and his wife are showing your children things that are against the law, there's nothing we can do."

Hope said, "No, but as soon as you think I've done something to him, you wanna arrest me."

The female officer replied, "Well, ma'am, the person who called us said you were hitting on somebody and causing a ruckus. There are laws prohibiting battery and disturbing the peace."

Hope said, "Well, I'm sorry for disturbing the peace, but that's all I'm sorry for. I barely touched him."

The officers looked at Lance.

Lance said, "I'm fine. I don't wanna press any charges. We'll work this out."

"Okay," the male officer replied. As he and the other officer turned to go back to their vehicle, he said, "You folks have a good evening."

Lance attempted to reason with Hope regarding the video situation, but as soon as the officers had pulled out of the driveway, she got into her car and drove away.

On the drive home, she looked at the road ahead of her through tears. Just a few years ago, her life had been so full and happy. Then suddenly, her world had been shattered. The hate she felt for Lance and Leeza had not diminished with time. She still hated them with every fiber of her being.

"Man, this is the life, isn't it?" Tristen said as he and Jon sat back with their fishing lines in the water.

"Yeah," Jon agreed. "So relaxing. Reminds me of when we were kids." A sparkle lit up his eyes. "Hey, do you remember when we were little and everybody knew how to ride a bike but me? I used to get so mad watching you and Torey and Terrell ride when I couldn't. Y'all had only one bicycle and had to take turns riding it. Remember the time Torey taught me to ride and you didn't know it till you saw me round the corner at y'all's house? You said, 'Dawg, Torey, you don' taught Jon how to ride. That's one more person we're gon' have to take turns sharing the bicycle with.'"

Tristen fell back laughing. "Yeah, I remember. I didn't want another person to have to split up my riding time with.

And once you learned, you never wanted to let us ride our own bicycle. Man, you were selfish."

"Aw, naw, man, that ain't even how it was."

"Yeah, right. You know it was. Hey, remember the li'l straw house we made in the woods?"

"Yeah, and when we went back the next day, we got mad when we saw the wind had destroyed it?"

"Yeah, you cried like a baby."

Jon fell into deep laughter. "Man, you crazy. I didn't cry. *You* cried."

"I don't remember me crying, but I remember you crying."

"You have selective memory."

The two friends shared another laugh.

Tristen happily expressed, "Those were the good ole days."

"Yeah," Jon agreed.

There was a slight pause.

Jon added, "Listen at us. We're still young and we sound like we're old men."

Tristen chuckled. "We do, don't we. But I guess that's what happens with aging. When you're a kid, time creeps. As you get older, it flies by. Sometimes you wish you could slow it down."

"Yeah. But as much as I miss my childhood, I don't wanna go back. I mean, look at me now. Soon I'll be marrying the woman I love, my best friend's sister. And I'm sitting here now with my best friend, enjoying life and talking about old times."

"I agree. We can't live in the past, but it's fun to think about it sometimes and enjoy talking about it. Just think—someday we'll be telling our children and grandchildren about our past lives." As an afterthought, Tristen added, "And I can't wait to tell yours about some of the things you used to do. For all those times you got Momma to bring up my past, I'm gonna get you."

Jon slapped his hand to his forehead. "Oh, naw. Boy, am I in for it."

Tristen stated with a short laugh, "You know it."

Chapter 13

The month of July wore on as the weather got hotter. Tyla and Jon were busy planning the wedding and dividing their time between themselves and their family.

On this last Sunday of the month, instead of everyone assembling at Myah's, Tristen had planned a casual afternoon gathering elsewhere. After church, their first stop was a nice neighborhood Caribbean restaurant with live music and dancing. Everyone got a thrill when Myah and Tristen danced. They saw Myah do moves they didn't know she had.

When Tristen escorted his mother back to her seat, Myah teased them, saying, "Y'all think just 'cause I'm older than y'all that I can't dance. I can get my groove on when I want to."

After lunch, they went to the aquarium where they spent the remainder of the afternoon.

Later that night, as Tyla oiled her mother's scalp in the

living room, Myah said, "I had a wonderful time today. God ain't gon' let me get old with you kids around. Today was the best time I've had in a while."

Tyla made a long part in her mother's hair, dipped her finger into the hair conditioner beside her on the sofa and smeared it onto her mother's scalp. "I'm glad you had a good time. I did, too. You know, I really appreciate how Tristen tries to keep the family together."

"Yeah. Me, too. I worry about him sometimes, though."

"Why, Momma? He's fine."

"I know. I just wish he could find a good woman to marry and settle down with. I want him to be happy."

"I believe he is happy."

"I believe he is, too. I just wish he had someone special to share his happiness with other than us."

"It'll happen one day, Momma. Tristen's a very unique person. He just hasn't found the right woman yet—one who'll appreciate him the way he deserves to be."

"Yeah. You're right. But you know, I'm a momma, and I still worry about y'all sometimes."

"You don't have to."

"I know I don't have to, but I do. It's all part of being a mother. You'll see one day, when you and Jon get married and start a family of your own."

The thought of raising a family with Jon sent Tyla's heart reeling. "Well, I just hope that I'm as good a mother as you are to us."

Tyla's expression was like a gentle caress to Myah's soul. "That's sweet, honey. I have a feeling you'll make a wonderful mother and wife to Jon. And Jon will be a good husband and father, too. You two were made for each other. It just took a lotta years and both of you growing up to discover it."

Tyla pondered her mother's words as she made another part in her hair. Her mother was right. Life was sweet, but having Jon by her side made it sweeter.

Another Sunday afternoon, and Hope was at her part-time job while her children were with Lance and Leeza. She despised the couple further for having more time and freedom to spend with her children than she did.

She didn't know how much longer she could keep up her routine. She felt she was killing herself physically, but she didn't know what else to do. She had to keep going in order to care for the material needs of herself and her children. But what about their spiritual needs?

As she stood behind the counter, ringing up her customers' products, she noticed and admired all the people who were coming into the store in their Sunday best, apparently having just come from church.

What good was it to spend your whole life working your fingers to the bone if you died in an instant out of God's favor. Didn't he say in his Word that if you put him first in your life that he would make sure you had what you needed? It had been a while since she'd taken in anything spiritual, but Hope remembered that, at least.

Then why wasn't she living her life as though she believed it? Didn't the Bible also say that God didn't lie? Why was she so afraid to try to serve him and put him to the test to see if he would keep his promise of providing for her and her family?

She began to envy not just Lance and Leeza but all the people she knew in the world who seemed to be so happy and content with their lives, not just in a material sense, but in a spiritual one.

Hope soon realized that she couldn't be like them because her circumstances were such that she had to put all her energies and efforts into taking care of her family. She didn't have time left for anything spiritual.

When she got home later that night, the house was quiet. For the first time in a while, she felt utterly alone. In the past, she had somehow willed herself from wanting or needing anybody. But at this very moment, she wished she had someone to come home to after a hard day's work. Someone who would take her in his arms and tell her that things were going to be okay. Someone to wipe away her tears when she couldn't hold them back.

She felt herself bearing down under pressure and she couldn't do that. She had to keep herself strong in order to continue going.

She went into the bathroom and started running her bathwater. When she slipped down into the warm, sudsy water and sank back against the tub, her tears slid down her cheeks and mixed with the water.

Chapter 14

What had happened to summer? Fall was less than two weeks away. Hope felt like she had aged twenty years within the last six weeks. With Brandon back in school and not working, she really missed his contributions, no matter how small, toward paying for his car. One thing they had to celebrate, though, was just last week, his caseworker had given him his papers releasing him from his three-month probationary period. Although he seemed to be doing all right in school, there were still times when he appeared sad and withdrawn.

Hope worked even harder, putting in extra hours at the Junction in order to provide materially for her family. Some days took their toll on her more than others. She had a host of emotions that she didn't know how to deal with. Not only was she physically exhausted, but the hatred she continued to feel for Lance and Leeza left her mentally and emotionally drained.

She had again started to question the need for spiritual guidance in her life. She couldn't understand why. She couldn't remember the last time she'd prayed. Before all the chaos in her life, earnest, heartfelt prayers had come so easily to her. Now, she couldn't even form the first sentence to one. Hopelessness and despair crowded all around her.

As Hope sat at her computer, she felt a sudden tightening in her chest. She'd been experiencing the discomfort all morning but had kept trying to ignore it. She had her hand to her chest when she heard a cheery voice from behind her.

"Good morning."

Hope quickly removed her hand from her chest and turned slightly to see Tyla in her cubicle. "Mornin'," she mumbled.

She struggled to ignore the discomfort in her chest while Tyla attempted to engage her in conversation. Hope breathed a sigh of relief when she finally walked away.

Tyla was starving. The bagel with cream cheese she'd eaten for breakfast hadn't satisfied her appetite. As she trekked at a fast pace through the hospital's parking deck toward her car, she saw something up ahead of her that appeared to be a person lying on the ground. As she got closer, she realized it was a woman lying on her side, her back toward Tyla.

Panic rippled through Tyla's body as she felt the adrenaline begin to pump faster and faster. *What to do? What to do?*

Tyla quickly recalled the first three steps in an emergency—check, call and care.

Check the scene and check the victim. Tyla examined the area around the woman to see if there were any signs of danger. When she detected none, she approached the woman, dropping her pocketbook off her shoulder to the ground. She began shaking the woman, asking in a loud voice, "Are you okay?" When she didn't respond, Tyla gently pulled the woman onto her back. When she recognized the woman as Hope, paralysis quickly set in. *No, it can't be!* Tyla tried to thrust her fear aside and recall what to do next. She had to check the victim for signs of life—pulse, breathing and the rise and fall of the chest. She sensed none of them. Panic ripped at her again as she promptly recalled the next emergency step.

Call for help. Tyla quickly reached over and grabbed her cell phone from her purse, dialing 911. She gave the operator all the information she needed. The operator asked if she knew how to do rescue breathing.

Care for the victim. Tyla blew two breaths into Hope's mouth. Then she looked, listened and felt for breathing for ten seconds. There were still no signs of life in Hope. Next, she delivered one rescue breath every five seconds, a total of twelve breaths a minute. She checked again for breathing.

Tyla grabbed her cell phone off the ground and advised the operator that Hope still wasn't breathing. The operator asked if she knew CPR. She stated that she did but wasn't sure if she remembered how to administer it properly. The operator told her to give the victim four sets of two rescue breaths and fifteen chest compressions and then to check the victim's pulse. If the victim still was not breathing, continue to repeat the cycle and check her pulse after each one. She also advised Tyla that if she lost count, not to worry but to continue administering CPR until Hope had a pulse or medical help had arrived.

Tyla began administering CPR. After the first four sets, she checked for a pulse. When she found none, she started a second set. She was getting tired, but she didn't stop. After the second set, she got a pulse, although Hope was still unconscious. Tyla grabbed her cell phone again and advised the operator of Hope's condition. The operator assured her that the staff at Mercy had been notified and medical help was on the way.

As soon as the operator ended the call, Tyla saw hospital staff coming from all directions of the parking deck. Hope was put on a stretcher and rushed to the elevator.

A coworker stayed behind with Tyla and accompanied her to the E.R. Tyla's nerves were shot. None of them could believe this had happened to one of their own. Tyla kept insisting on seeing Hope. The E.R. supervisor and a few other staff members were finally able to get Tyla to sit down. She was shaking like a leaf as she nervously relayed to them what had happened. She couldn't stop sobbing. Thoughts of her father and seeing Hope lying in the parking lot lifeless had overtaken her.

Tyla's supervisor offered to take her home, but Tyla refused. The supervisor instructed another staff member to look up Tyla's emergency contact information. Myah was at the hospital in less than twenty minutes. When she saw her daughter, it was as though they were reliving Maurice's death all over again. Myah pulled Tyla into her arms and held her tight. When she tried to get Tyla to come home with her, Tyla wouldn't budge. So Myah stayed with her in the E.R.'s waiting room while they awaited word on Hope's condition.

Chapter 15

About an hour after Hope had been brought to the emergency room, Tyla and Myah had seen a man, a woman and three teenagers, a boy and two girls, rush in and inquire about Hope. Tyla remembered the two young girls from the mall and figured the young man was Hope's son or some close relative. But who were the man and woman?

Another hour later, the E.R. supervisor informed Tyla that Hope had been admitted to a room. When Tyla asked to see her, the supervisor advised her that only immediate family were being allowed visitation at the moment. Only then was Myah able to get Tyla to finally go home.

On the ride, Tyla lamented, "Momma, I was so scared when I saw her lying there in the parking lot. When I started administering CPR, I just knew I was gonna mess up and do something wrong. All I knew was I had to do something."

Myah smiled and patted her daughter's hand. "And you

did good, honey. The emergency medical technicians and hospital staff said if it wasn't for your quick thinking, she probably wouldn't have made it. They even said the 911 operator mentioned how quick you were on your feet."

Tyla leaned her head back and closed her eyes. "I don't ever want to go through that again. I'm not sure I want to be a nurse anymore."

Myah tried to think of something encouraging to say while Tyla rattled on.

"People's lives being in your hands all the time, that's a very heavy burden to carry. I don't know if I can handle that kind of pressure."

"I think you'd handle it very well. Look at how you handled it today. You gained hands-on experience. Now you know what you'd do in an emergency situation."

Tyla raised her head and looked at her mother. "But I was a nervous wreck."

Myah gave Tyla a look filled with tenderness. "How else were you supposed to feel? Feeling nervous, especially about life-and-death situations, doesn't make you weak. It shows your humility, that you're relying on a higher power and not yourself. God is the one who gives us that power beyond what is normal to make it in this world and do the things we have to do. Tyla, you have such a kind heart. You care so much about people. I see that, but I can't see your heart the way God sees it. We're not God, no matter what position on this earth we hold. We need him to help us through those difficult times."

Myah reached over, put her hand on her daughter's leg

and lovingly shook it. "Girl, the Lord was with you in that parking lot. Have you thought about that? His Holy Spirit was with you. How do you think you were able to remember what to do to help your coworker? Just remember, baby, that even if we fall as we sometimes will, it doesn't mean God has abandoned us. He allows us to be tested, but he's always there for us. Just like a loving parent. When we fall down, he picks us up, kisses us where it hurts and encourages us to keep going."

Tyla quietly contemplated her mother's words of wisdom and slowly began to feel a little better.

Chapter 16

Tyla tried, without success, for the next three days to see Hope. Much to Tyla's surprise, a member of the hospital staff called the next day to tell her that Hope wanted to see her. When she got there, Hope's daughters were visiting.

Hope looked frail and weak. Tyla leaned down and gave her a hug. She straightened up and asked, "How are you?"

Hope responded, "I've been better, but I'm okay." Looking at the teenagers, she asked, "Do you remember my daughters, Ashlee and Brittney?"

Tyla looked at them and smiled. "Of course, I do. Hey. How are y'all doing?"

"Fine," the girls answered.

Tyla heard Brittney whisper to her sister, "I told you that was her."

Hope gave her daughters a stern look. "What are y'all whispering about?"

Brittney grabbed the magazine they'd been looking at earlier from the windowsill. She flipped through a few pages and took the publication to her mother. Pointing at a pretty young woman in a blue-jeans ad, she stated as she pointed at Tyla, "That's her." Looking at Tyla, she asked, "Isn't it?"

Tyla appeared humble as she captured a glimpse of herself in the ad. "Yes. Do you like it?"

Ashlee had come around to join her sister by the side of the bed.

Brittney answered, "Yes. You're sooo pretty."

Hope was overwhelmed with shock and amazement. She'd had no idea that Tyla was also a fashion model. She watched the exchange between her daughters and Tyla.

Ashlee said, "I wish I could be a model."

Brittney added, "Me, too."

Tyla's face lit up the entire room. "You could do catalog work or model clothes in stores for teens."

The girls' eyes glowed radiantly.

Brittney said, "Could we? That'd be great."

Ashlee eagerly asked, "How would we get started?"

Hope had come so close to dying, but she'd been given a second chance. The hospital staff had told her that Tyla was the one who had found her unconscious in the hospital parking deck and administered CPR after she'd suffered a heart attack. She didn't want to become Tyla's bosom buddy. She just wanted to utter a quick thank-you so she could get on with life with her children.

Hope pressed the button to raise the head part of her

bed. "Girls, go check on your brother and your daddy in the cafeteria."

After the teenagers left the room, Hope wasted no time in getting straight to the point.

"Everybody told me what you did to help me. How you administered CPR and saved my life."

Tyla humbly stated, "I only did what I was trained to do."

Hope continued, "I appreciate what you did. I know I haven't been nice to you, but we're two different people. I'm trying to raise my children. I don't have time to go around trying to be everybody's friend. I'm also trying to keep my kids' feet on the ground so don't fill their heads with big ideas about modeling careers."

"I wasn't trying to fill their heads with anything. They expressed a desire to model and I was just trying to give them some encouragement. But if it bothers you, I won't mention it to them again." She paused, then added, "Can we change the subject? I've been really worried about you. I'm glad you're okay."

Hope gave Tyla a questioning gaze. "Do you treat everybody the way you treat me?"

Tyla returned her look. "I don't know what you mean."

"Why are you always so nice to me?"

"That's just who I am."

"Why did you help me in the parking deck?"

"Because I care about you."

"Why?"

Tyla was trying not to get frustrated with all the ridiculous questions Hope was hurling at her. She felt like she was being interrogated for some crime. Was it wrong to show concern for people?

"Because I care about people."

"You're odd. I don't mean in a bad way. You're different. I've never met anyone like you before. Always happy. Are you ever sad?"

"Yes, I am."

"You never show it."

"That doesn't mean I don't ever feel it."

"How can you be sad and not show it?"

"Laughing, talking and smiling are *my* way of dealing with it."

Hope was about to fling another question at Tyla when her daughters came in with Brandon and their father. Hope made quick introductions before Tyla politely said goodbye.

Tyla still couldn't figure out her coworker. The exchange between them a few minutes ago in Hope's hospital room was the longest conversation they'd had that wasn't work related. All Tyla could figure was that Hope was obviously a woman with some deep-rooted issues.

Hope had been out of the hospital for two weeks. Though she was eager to get back to both of her jobs, her physician would not release her to return for another two weeks and only on a part-time basis at the hospital. Not only that, he'd advised her to give up her part-time job at the Junction. She was grateful to still be alive, but she didn't care what the doctor said. She had a family to support. Neither he nor anybody else was going to pay her bills for her.

It was almost one o'clock Saturday morning and Brandon still had not gotten home. His curfew was eleven o'clock. She'd gotten him a cell phone in case of emergencies, but every time she called him, she got his voice mail. She'd called Lance several times asking if he'd seen him or heard from him. He hadn't but assured her that he would go out in search of him. She kept picturing Brandon lying on the side of the road somewhere hurt or dead, but she and Lance had decided not to call the police this time because they didn't want him in trouble again with the juvenile authorities.

At twenty-five minutes after one, Hope heard Brandon entering the apartment. She quickly jumped out of bed, ran to the living room and flipped on the light. Brandon's big eyes, eyes like his father's, stared back at her.

Hope didn't want to wake the girls and tried not to yell. "Where have you been?"

"Out with my friends. You said I could go."

"Brandon, your curfew is eleven o'clock. It's almost one-thirty." Hope glanced at the clock on the wall. "Where have you been?"

"I told you, hanging out with my friends."

"Hanging out where?"

"Just out."

"Oh, so you're not gon' tell me where you've been. You been in some kind of devilment?"

"No, we were just hanging out."

"But you can't tell me where?"

When Brandon didn't respond, Hope held out her hands. "Gimme the keys."

Brandon's eyes grew more huge. "My car keys?"

"Yeah, your car keys. What keys do you think I'm talking about. Hand 'em here."

"But, Mama—"

"Don't *but, Mama* me. Give 'em here."

Reluctantly, Brandon handed over the keys and stormed away.

Hope yelled after him, "When you start acting like you got some sense, you can have 'em back."

Before going back to bed, she called Lance and informed him that their son was home. She also gave Lance a lecture on how he needed to speak to Brandon about his negative attitude and behavior.

As Hope lay in bed, she could feel the tension rising in her chest. Brandon used to be such a sweet, innocent child. Now he was becoming unruly. The more she thought about how sad her life had become, the angrier she grew at Lance and Leeza.

On Monday, Tyla called Tristen at work to see if he was free for lunch.

When Tyla placed her order at McDonald's, Tristen asked, "What's with the salad? You tryin' to lose weight? You're already no bigger'n an ant."

Tyla made a face and said, "I've got less than a month before the wedding. I've got to be able to fit into my dress." When her tray was placed in front of her, she said, "I'll get us a table."

She waited for her brother to say his blessing after he'd

joined her. When he was finished, she said, "I need to ask you something. Have you noticed Jon acting differently lately?"

"No. Why?" Tristen took a bite of his Big Mac.

"Well, he just seems different all of a sudden. Every time I try to talk to him about the wedding, he changes the subject."

Tristen dismissed his sister's notions. "Ah, that's just prewedding jitters."

Tyla put her hands on her sides and gave her brother a stern look. "Now, I don't know how I'm supposed to take that. Do you think he has a reason to be nervous about marrying me?"

Tristen laughed. "No, you're every man's dream. Strong yet feminine. Adventurous yet caring with a sense of humor. I wish I could meet somebody like you."

Tyla gave him a cynical stare. "You could if you'd stop being so nitpicky and running away every girl you meet. I don't know of any man who has to have everything perfect like you."

Her tone turned serious as she recalled her mother's recent concerns about her brother. Echoing her mother, she warmly expressed, "I worry about you."

"Why?"

"I worry about you being lonely."

"Who said I was lonely?"

"Well, you just said you wished you could meet somebody."

"Yes, I did, but I didn't say I was lonely." Tristen bit into his Big Mac again.

"I just want you to find someone who will really love you and be good to you. You deserve that."

"Thanks, but I'm not lonely. There's a huge difference between being alone and being lonely. Yes, I'm alone in the physical sense as far as the opposite sex goes, but I'm never lonely. I've got twenty-nine kids on my caseload who keep me busy in and out of the office, plus a family, which includes my little sister who keeps bugging me about finding a girlfriend."

Tyla rolled her eyes at him.

"Seriously, I'm not lonely. You're making it sound like I'm Momma's homely-looking child who can't get a girlfriend to save his life. Do I look *that* bad?"

Tyla released a little laugh. "You're aw-right. Even if I am your sister."

She had eaten every drop of her salad and was still hungry. If they hadn't been in public, she would have picked up the bowl and licked the salad dressing drippings from it. She tried casually to look at the last small bite of hamburger and three French fries Tristen had left.

She was about to ask if she could have them when a McDonald's employee approached them with a tray full of their spicy chicken sandwich cut up into big-size samples in small containers.

The young man asked, "Have you tried a sample of our spicy chicken sandwich?"

Before the employee or Tristen knew it, Tyla had grabbed a sample from the tray.

"Thank you," Tyla said, grinning.

Tristen held up his hand, saying, "No, thank you. I'm fine."

As soon as the young man had walked away, Tristen said, "Dawg, girl. I don't think I've ever seen you go after food that fast. Your hand went by me like a streak of lightning."

Tyla let out a soft chuckle as she wolfed down the last bite of the sandwich. She washed it down with a guzzle of her bottled water.

"Pick at me all you want to. That salad was good, but I'm still hungry."

Tristen shook his head. "The things you women do to keep from gaining a little weight. Now back to Jon. You said he's been acting strange lately? Do you want me to talk to him? See if anything's going on?"

Tyla shook her head. "Nah, that's okay. I'm sure everything's fine. It's probably just me. Hey, wanna hang out with me tonight?"

Tristen shot her a questioning look, then gazed around the restaurant.

Tyla asked, "What are you looking at?"

"I'm looking for Jon. I thought maybe he'd just walked in and you were talking to him 'cause you hardly ever have time for your big brother anymore. I'm surprised you could fit me into your schedule today."

Tyla rolled her eyes. "Oh, hush." She straightened in her seat and said, "So tell me, what are y'all planning to do Saturday at Jon's bachelor party?"

Tristen's expression became guarded. "Somebody sure is nosy. None of your business. Ain't nobody asking what's gonna be going on at your li'l lingerie party Saturday."

Tyla's eyes increased in size. She leaned toward Tristen and whispered, "How'd you know it's a lingerie shower?"

"You know how you and Momma are." Tristen put his fingers together and pressed them up and down against his thumb several times. "Yak. Yak. I heard you talking."

Tyla frowned. "You didn't have to listen, nosy. Well, I'm glad you and Torey and Terrell are the ones giving Jon his party. That way, I know it'll be clean and decent."

Tristen propped his elbow onto the table and began rubbing his chin with his fingers, a devilish grin covering his entire face. "Who told you we were gonna keep it clean and decent? We want him to have a good time, don't we?"

Tyla made a small fist and knocked his elbow off the table. "Tristen, you wouldn't. You do and I'll kill you."

Tristen started laughing. "Girl, relax. You know I'm just kidding." He observed the look of ease that came over her and teased, "You okay? You looked like you were about to pass out."

Tyla said again, "Oh, hush," just as the young man with the tray of chicken sandwich samples approached their table again.

He asked, "Have y'all tried our chicken sandwich samples?"

Tristen tried to roll his eyes discreetly and said, "Yes."

Tyla added, "But you don't mind if we have another one, do you?"

The young man said, "No, I don't mind."

As soon as the words were out of his mouth, Tyla had grabbed another sample. "Thank you."

"You're welcome."

When the young man had gone, Tristen said, "Now, he know he was just at this table a few minutes ago with that tray. He ain't slick. If he comes back over here, hold that engagement ring up in his face where he can see it. I could be your boyfriend for all he knows."

Tyla cracked a smile. "Ooh. Gross. You need to stop."

Tristen eyed her half-eaten sample. "You should've left that salad alone and just ordered the whole chicken sandwich. By the time you get through sampling, you'll have eaten a whole one."

Tyla put the rest of the sample into her mouth and popped his arm.

Chapter 17

Friday afternoon, Tyla stopped by to visit Hope on her way home from work. One more week and Hope could return to her job, the doctor had assured her this morning when she'd gone for her follow-up appointment. Eager to get back to work, she had been trying to do everything he'd suggested, including focusing on her own health and well-being. It wasn't easy.

She'd noticed since she'd begun recuperating from the heart attack that her feelings about her spirituality had resurfaced. For some reason, her life had been spared. This time. She wondered why.

She was beginning to see the need to reestablish her relationship with God but had not a clue as to how or where to begin. At times, she felt confused because she was no longer sure about what she needed or wanted. Sometimes she wanted to be alone; other times, she felt the desire to have a close friend by her side. But she had no close friends. Even if she did, could they be trusted not to betray her?

All Hope had were her children, and the oldest one she felt she was losing. She had thought that getting Brandon the car would be a motivating factor to his doing better in school and not having such a bad attitude toward her. What it had done was had quite the opposite effect. He'd told her again recently that he wanted to go live with his father. She couldn't understand why Brandon wanted to live with him after what he'd done to their family. As she tried to regain her son, her anger and resentment toward Lance and Leeza continued to grow in her heart like a well-watered plant in fine soil.

Hope had allowed Brandon to drive him and his sisters to their high school football game tonight. Tyla had stopped at Wendy's and gotten her and Hope some grilled chicken sandwiches and caesar salads for supper. Myah had shared with her that it was important that Hope eat healthy foods in order to get her strength back and maintain good health.

Hope sat at the kitchen table and watched Tyla prepare their plates. Hope observed in wonder how at ease Tyla seemed in her kitchen. She would have been fine with eating the food from the restaurant wrappers and containers it had come in, but Tyla had insisted on making it homey and had even promised to clean up afterward.

Hope would never admit it to Tyla, but she was beginning to like her. Tyla seemed genuine, but Hope still didn't know whether or not she could trust her. Leeza had also been what Hope had considered a true friend.

Tyla brought two plates to the table and placed one in

front of Hope. "I didn't bring any sodas since I know you're trying to eat healthy. What would you like to drink?"

Hope managed a slight smile. "Water is fine. There's some bottled water in the fridge." Pointing to a corner cupboard, she added, "The glasses are in that cabinet. Thank you."

"You're welcome," Tyla said as she turned and headed for the cupboard. After she'd poured their water, she joined Hope at the table and said, "Excuse me," before bowing her head to say her blessing.

Hope tried not to stare and bit off a piece of her sandwich.

When Tyla was done, she took a bite of hers before looking at Hope and smiling. "So how was your day?"

"It was okay. I went to the doctor this morning."

Tyla expected her to go on. When she didn't, she asked, "Did you get a good report?"

Hope nodded as she chewed her food. "Yes. I can go back to work on the sixteenth. Part-time for the first couple of weeks." She almost mentioned her part-time job at the Junction and the fact that her doctor had encouraged her to give it up, but she'd decided against it.

Tyla smiled again as she straightened in her chair. "Well, I know you were glad to hear that since you've been talking about how you can't wait to go back. Are you taking it easy like he told you?" She took in a small portion of salad.

Much to her surprise, Hope found herself grinning and mellowing out somewhat. "Yes, ma'am." It was nice to have someone be concerned about her.

Tyla said, "I'm not trying to be bossy. I was just asking. As soon as we get through eating and I clean up the kitchen, I can help you with anything else you need done."

Hope liked having another adult around to talk to, even if the person was young enough to be her daughter. But despite Tyla's age, she was a very mature woman and Hope hadn't had anybody show this much concern for her since the breakup of her marriage. The thought of their broken home made her think of Brandon.

Tyla surveyed Hope's face. "Are you okay?"

There was a sadness in Hope's eyes. "I'm fine."

"Are you sure? You look like something's on your mind. Is there anything you want to talk about?"

Hope couldn't trust this young woman with anything personal. She had gotten accustomed to handling her problems on her own. She wasn't ready to start sharing her emotions with anyone after what she'd been through.

"I'm fine," she said again.

"Okay," Tyla responded. She stood and took her plate over to the sink. Then she turned around. "Are you through—"

Tyla saw Hope's hands clasped underneath her chin. Her eyes closed, tears streamed down her face. Tyla rushed to her and leaned down. Putting her hand gently on Hope's shoulder, she asked, "Hope, what's wrong?"

Words would not come for Hope. She just sat there like a statue.

Tyla rubbed her hand gently up and down Hope's back. "Why are you crying?" She sensed that the only way to get Hope to open up to her was to assure her that she could talk to her. She grabbed the chair she'd been sitting on, pulled it closer to Hope and sat down facing her.

"You can talk to me, Hope, if you want to. Whatever it is, I may not be able to help, but I sure can listen. Maybe you'll feel better if you just talk about it. That's what I do when I'm feeling bad. I talk to my family. Even though the problem's sometimes still there, just talking to them helps."

Tyla couldn't think of anything else to say. When she went over to the paper towel holder to tear off a couple of sheets, she said a quick prayer to God to help her. She put the towels in Hope's hand and sat back down.

Hope opened her eyes and warmly expressed, "Thank you," as she wiped her face.

"You're welcome."

Hope clasped her hands again and laid them on the table, the wadded up paper towels still in her grasp. She looked at her hands. "I'm sorry."

"You don't have to apologize to me."

Bottom lip trembling, Hope said, "It's my son, Brandon. He's seventeen now. He wants to move in with his father. I feel like I'm losing him. This is his last year of high school and his grades are suffering. I think he's still hurting over the divorce. I don't know what to do anymore."

An idea immediately popped into Tyla's head. "My brother works with juveniles. Maybe he can help. Do you want him to talk to Brandon?"

When Hope looked at Tyla, a ray of hope shined in her eyes. "You don't think he'd mind?"

"No, he won't mind. He loves his job and loves working

with kids. I don't know if he'll be able to do it this weekend though. He and my brothers are throwing my fiancé a bachelor party, but I'll talk to him and get back with you."

Hope managed a smile. "That'd be great."

Tyla had another great idea. "Hey, my momma, sister-in-law and future sister-in-law are throwing me a lingerie shower tomorrow. I know it's short notice, but I'd love it if you came. Do you think you'll feel up to it? It's gonna be at the Caribbean restaurant in town. I'll pick you up. You can ride with me. It'll give you an opportunity to get out and have some fun."

It sounded like fun, but Hope had some misgivings. "I don't know. I think I'm a little too old to be hanging out at a lingerie shower with you and your young friends."

Tyla jumped up from her seat. "What are you talking about? My momma, of all people, will be there. Y'all are probably the same age or close to it."

Hope found herself giggling. "Your momma's really gonna be at your lingerie shower. If I was in your shoes, I'd die."

"Yeah, that's how I felt when I first found out about it, but my family's like that. Always doing something crazy."

Tyla's family sounded like a lot of fun. Hope had the first hearty laugh she'd had in a long while.

The next day, Tyla stopped by Tristen's apartment after her and Jon's morning ride. She followed him from room to room, yelling over the noise of the vacuum cleaner.

"So you'll do it?" she yelled. When he didn't answer, she pulled the cord from the wall outlet in his bedroom.

Tristen turned on her. "What'd you do that for?"

"You didn't answer me. I asked you if you'll do it. I need an answer."

"Tyla, why do you always do this to me? Isn't it enough that I've got almost thirty kids on my caseload at work to deal with without you going out soliciting for more?"

Tyla put her hands on her hips. "You know you want to. You know how much you love kids and will do anything to help 'em."

"Yeah, you know that, too. That's why you're always bugging me about everybody's kids like I don't already have enough to do. How old is he again?"

"Seventeen. He's a high school senior."

"What kind of trouble is he having?"

Tyla rolled her eyes in silence. Then she said, "I already told you."

"Look. Do you want me to help the boy or not? I didn't hear half of what you said trailing behind me with this vacuum cleaner going. What's his problem?"

"His parents are divorced. He's the only boy and the oldest child. His grades are suffering. His mom thinks his problems are mainly due to the divorce."

Tristen grunted, "Probably just needs a good old-fashioned butt whipping."

Tyla's mouth dropped open in shock. "Tristen, I can't believe you said that, especially since some of the kids you work with are physically abused."

"Some kids are physically abused, but sometimes a good butt whipping don't hurt none. I'm not talking about beating up on 'em. I'm talking about discipline. Momma and Daddy used to whip our behinds—well not yours with your li'l spoiled self."

Tyla narrowed her eyes at him.

Tristen went on, "They used to beat our behinds all the time and it didn't kill us. In fact, I think it made us better people. That's part of the problem with some of these kids today. Their parents pamper 'em and let 'em get away with murder."

"That's not fair. You don't even know him and you're judging him."

"I'm just giving you the facts."

"Well, I don't have time to stand here and listen to you deliver a sermon about the differences between kids today and kids thirty years ago."

Tristen's dark eyes pierced the space between them. "If I tell you I'll do it, will you get outta here and leave me alone?" His tone was noncommital. "I've still got some more cleaning to do before Jon's party tonight and you's got to go."

Tyla wasn't budging. "When can you do it? Tomorrow?"

"My Lord, girl. You're just not gon' give me a break, are you?"

Tyla folded her arms across her chest and stared at her brother.

"Yeah, yeah. Tomorrow afternoon around five o'clock?"

Tyla smiled. "Okay." She dropped her hands to her sides and gave her brother a peck on his left cheek.

"Don't be kissing on me," he uttered. "Will you get outta my way now?"

Tyla turned and walked away, waving over her shoulder, and saying, "I love you."

Tristen said, "I love you, too," before turning the vacuum cleaner back on.

The next morning, despite how tired she was from her lingerie shower, Tyla arose early for the nine-thirty worship service and attended with her mother.

Everyone had had a lot of fun at the shower. One of the best surprises was seeing some of her old friends from school whom she hadn't seen or talked with in a while. Her mother had gotten in touch with their parents and had been able to secure their phone numbers and addresses. It seemed like Hope had enjoyed herself, too. It made Tyla happy to see her smiling.

The day wore on and Tristen picked up Tyla promptly at a quarter before five and they headed for Hope's apartment. She'd been so afraid that he would be late or forget. Of course, the fact that she'd called him every hour and reminded him had probably helped considerably. On the way, Tyla questioned him about Jon's party the night before.

"Was my baby good last night?" Tyla asked teasingly, and a little seriously.

"Tyla, everything was cool. We had some good clean fun. No strippers or girls popping out of cakes. Don't you trust Jon or us, your own brothers?"

"Yeah, but I know how some of those parties can get out of hand."

Tristen gave his sister a quick glance. "All men aren't like that. And as for Jon, he's loyal, faithful and true. He loves you and he'd never do anything to hurt you."

Tyla suddenly felt embarrassed regarding her negative thinking. "I know."

She changed the subject, talking about school, her modeling and her job at the hospital. When they arrived at Hope's apartment complex, Tristen found a convenient parking space. They chatted as they made their way up the sidewalk to Hope's front door. Tyla knocked three times. The door was opened promptly by a young girl who gave them a friendly greeting and invited them inside.

Tyla said, "Ashlee, right?"

"Right."

They followed Ashlee into the living room.

Tyla said, "It's good to see you again."

"You, too."

Tyla motioned toward Tristen. "This is my brother, Tristen. Tristen, this is Ashlee, Hope's daughter."

Tristen and Ashlee said hello and shook hands before the three of them took a seat.

Ashlee said, "Mama will be out in a minute. She asked me to keep you entertained till she gets here."

The three of them chatted. Ashlee was filling them in on school when Hope appeared.

"Hello," Hope greeted them.

Tristen stood and turned to greet her. Their eyes met and locked. He was getting the feeling that he was in the twilight zone as a phenomenal sensation overcame him.

Tyla began, "Tristen, this is—"

"Hope," Tristen whispered.

Hope wanted to run and hide when she saw who it was. But her feet were cemented to the floor and he wouldn't let go of her hand.

Tyla said, "Yes. Hope, this is my brother, Tristen."

Hope finally managed to say hello, but nothing else would come out.

Tyla wondered why the two of them had suddenly turned into zombies. After several more seconds, she stepped in, grabbed their hands and pried them apart. "Okay. That's enough of that. Are y'all okay?"

Tristen stepped back. "Ah, yeah." He returned to his seat.

Tyla and Hope took a seat. Hope remained speechless.

Tristen couldn't take his eyes off Hope. "So how've you been?"

Hope tried to appear casual. "Okay."

Tristen asked, "So how are things at the store?"

Tyla had a puzzled expression on her face as she looked from one to the other.

Hope answered, "Fine."

Suddenly, Tyla held up her hand and said, "Hold up. What's going on here?" Waving her hand from one to the other, she asked, "Do you two know each other?"

Hope looked more embarrassed than before. "Ah, kind of."

Tyla just stared at Hope. When Hope gave no further explanation, Tyla looked at her brother.

Tristen explained, "We know each other from the Junction where she works."

Tyla vaguely remembered Tristan telling her about some woman at the store who'd gotten him and some other customers wet when she was watering the plants. She pointed her thumb backward at Hope. "You mean Hope's the woman from the Junction you told me about?"

Tristen nodded as a grin covered his entire face.

Hope wanted to crawl underneath the chair she was sitting on. She could just imagine the horrible stories brother and sister shared with each other about her. She'd treated them both so unkindly, and now here she was asking them to help her with Brandon. She wouldn't blame either of them if they just got up right now and walked out the door.

She was shocked when Tristen asked, "Is your son—Brandon—agreeable to talking with me?"

Hope honestly answered, "Well, he wasn't crazy about the idea at first, but he finally agreed. A couple of months ago, he was on a three-month probationary period through the juvenile justice system."

When she said that, it triggered another memory in Tristen's brain. "Who was his caseworker?"

Hope answered, "A woman named Dianne Beedles."

Tristen couldn't believe it. "She works in my office."

"Really?" Hope said.

Tyla sat watching the interchange between the two, not believing all that had transpired.

Tristen said, "I never saw the two of you in the office, but then, I could've been out or in my office when you came in." Suddenly, his brain triggered another memory. "Then again, maybe I did see you."

Hope said, "Maybe you did. I don't know."

"You don't remember? Y'all were leaving the office one day as I was coming in. You almost knocked me down with the door," Tristen added teasingly. "There was a man with you, too."

Hope couldn't hide her displeasure. "My ex-husband, Brandon's father."

Tristen continued, "Even that day, I had the feeling I'd seen you somewhere before but couldn't remember where." He let out a short laugh. "This is so funny. I can't believe it. Seems like every encounter I've had with you, I've come close to getting my head knocked off every time. You almost ran me over in the parking lot that day when you were trying to get away from me when I saw you sleeping. You watered me down in the garden shop and got pretty angry when I asked if I could join you on your break."

Tyla had the most confused look on her face. Everything her brother had just described sounded like something one would see in a movie.

Hope suddenly sensed what a wonderful sense of humor Tristen had. Despite how she'd treated him, he was sitting here in her living room laughing about it. The next thing she knew, she was rolling over in laughter with him and Tyla.

When their laughter finally subsided, Tristen straightened up and said regarding Hope, "So she can smile."

Hope felt like she'd been reborn. She hadn't really smiled or laughed in so long that she'd forgotten how good it felt.

Chapter 18

Monday afternoon, Tyla and Jon went on their usual horse-back ride. She had noticed that he still did not seem like himself. When he asked if they could cut short their ride, more anxiety set in.

On the drive back to her house, Tyla asked, "What's wrong?"

He was silent for a moment. Then he gave her a sad look and uttered, "We need to talk."

Tyla turned slightly in her seat and stared at him. He looked back at the road in front of them.

"What about?" she asked, her heart pounding. Something was terribly wrong. She'd never seen him look so sad or serious.

"We'll talk when we get to your house."

Tyla straightened herself in her seat and looked out her window. Neither of them said anything more on the rest of the drive. Once inside, she firmly gripped his hand in hers and led him to the sofa in the living room where they usually sat.

Tyla stayed on the edge of the chair and looked at him, his hand still in hers. "What's wrong?" Her heart was beating faster. "I have a feeling it's not something good. What is it?"

Jon pulled himself closer to the chair's edge, faced her, and cupped the right side of her face with his left hand. "I love you. You know that, don't you?"

All Tyla could do was nod.

Jon continued, "I always have and I always will. I want you to know that."

Tyla's voice was weak and shaky when she spoke. "Jon, you're scaring me. What is it?"

Jon took his hand from her face and grasped her hands in his. Tears began to pour from the corners of his eyes. They splattered onto the powder-blue shirt he was wearing and left small, dark wet spots.

Tyla was about to ask him why he was crying when he said, "I did something wrong. Something terrible and I have to tell you."

She was scared to ask, but she had to know what it was. "What'd you do?"

The words were stuck in his throat. It hurt him too much to say them and he knew they would pain Tyla even more when she heard them.

Tyla placed a delicate hand to his cheek and assured him, "Whatever it is, baby, you can tell me. What is it?"

The sight of him crying sent cold shivers up and down her

spine. She'd never seen him cry before except at her father's funeral, but even then, it wasn't as sorrowful as this. She wondered what terrible thing he had done to cause him so much grief. She couldn't imagine anything so bad.

Tyla put her hand on his back and tried to soothe away whatever was bothering him. "Honey, you've got to try to relax so you can talk to me."

Jon didn't want to tell her, but his conscience wouldn't allow him to keep silent any longer. The mere thought of what he had done and was about to tell her made him feel as though his insides were being ripped out.

Suddenly, he cried out, "I slept with another woman."

Surely her ears were playing tricks on her. Tyla twitched her head and, looking at him, said, "What?"

Jon openly wept more. "I didn't mean to. It just happened."

Tyla almost knocked him to the floor when she jumped up. She glared down at him. "Are you telling me you had sex with another woman?"

Jon propelled himself from the chair. "Yes, but it only happened once, Tyla. I'm so sorry."

Tyla heard herself scream, "I don't care how many times it happened! What matters is that it happened at all."

Jon said, "I don't want to hurt you, but I had to tell you."

Tyla sat back down and covered her face with her hands. "I don't believe this is happening." Dropping her hands onto her lap, she probed, "What were you thinking? We're getting married in less than a month."

Jon sat back down beside her. "Baby, I'm so sorry. I didn't mean for this to happen."

Tyla's head was whirling. She glared at him. "Who is she?"

His bottom lip quivered. "It doesn't matter."

Tyla jumped up again and turned on him. "I wanna know who she is. Here, I've been saving myself for you just like I thought you were doing for me and you went out and slept with someone else. I wanna know who she is."

Jon looked up at her with sad eyes. "A coworker. We've been working on a research project together."

"When did it happen?" Tyla demanded.

He didn't want to share any more with her than he had to. He had no intention of trying to shift the blame elsewhere for his selfish actions. "About a month ago." It had actually been the day that Tyla had been upset about her coworker's heart attack when he had wanted to take her out and she'd refused. When she'd encouraged him to go out and have some fun, he'd come across his coworker Gabriella at a bar and one thing had led to another.

Tyla's face was wet with hot tears. "Why, Jon? Why'd you do it? Were you so consumed with lust that you couldn't wait for us to get married?"

"I tried to wait, Tyla. You don't know how hard I tried."

They were silent for several seconds.

"I thought I could go on with the wedding and not tell you, but my conscience kept beating me up. I couldn't do that to you."

Tyla glared at him and snapped, "No, but you could sleep around on me." She had never gotten this angry at anyone and she didn't like the feeling. It had totally changed her personality.

"Tyla, I wasn't sleeping around. I told you it only happened once."

Despondency engulfed her. "How am I supposed to trust you now? How do I know you won't do it again after we're married?"

His next words threw her for another loop. Jon eyed Tyla pitifully. "We can't get married."

Her eyes grew huge. "What d'you mean, we can't get married? If either of us say that, shouldn't it be *me?* You've hurt *me,* but I still love you and I still want us to get married."

Jon decided to stand up. He'd finally gained the courage to stare into her innocent eyes. "Tyla, I can't marry you after what I did. My conscience won't let me and I don't feel that I'm ready for marriage."

"You can't be serious. You and I have been lifelong friends. We finally realized we were in love with each other and decided to get married. I mailed our wedding invitations Saturday. We've made all these wedding plans together. My brothers just gave you a bachelor party and my family gave me a bridal shower. I can't believe you're doing this." She took his hands in hers. "Jon, we can work this out. I don't want to lose you. I love you."

He touched his hand to her cheek. "I still love you, too, Tyla. That's why I can't marry you. You deserve better and I've got to let you go."

Tyla choked back more tears and whispered, "Let me go? I don't want you to let me go."

Jon whispered one last time, "I'll always love you." When he walked out the door, he felt a huge burden on his heart.

* * *

The house was quiet when Myah got home later that evening. Perhaps Tyla and Jon were still out riding although they were usually back by now. It was almost eight o'clock. Myah walked quietly down the hall. Tyla's bedroom door was closed. She always left it open when she wasn't home. Myah was about to knock when she thought she heard faint cries coming from within. With her hand balled into a tight fist against her chest, she listened intently. When she heard crying again, she knocked on the door four times.

"Tyla." Myah waited several seconds and knocked three more times. "Tyla, are you in there? Is something wrong? Are you crying?" She stood at the door for a few more seconds. "Tyla, open the door, please, or talk to me. Baby, what's the matter?"

Myah finally heard Tyla's muffled sorrowful voice.

"Momma, I can't talk right now. I just wanna be alone for a while. Okay?"

Myah turned and walked away. The only thing she knew to do was call Tristen. It only took him about fifteen minutes to get there and another five to get Tyla to unlock her bedroom door so he could enter.

Tristen watched his sister plop down onto the bed and curl up in a fetal position. He followed her and sat on the bed's edge.

"Tyla, what's wrong? Momma said you're upset about something and won't talk to her. Will you talk to me? You and I have always been able to talk about anything. What's wrong?"

Within an instant, Tyla had pulled herself up and wrapped her arms around her brother, her tears soaking his shirt.

"Jon called off the wedding," she lamented.

Outside in the hallway, Myah covered her mouth with her hand and leaned her back against the wall for support.

Tristen couldn't believe what he'd just heard. He stiffened for a moment. He held his sister tighter and tried not to sound shocked when he asked, "Why'd he do that?"

Tyla cried, "He slept with one of his coworkers."

Myah's legs began to feel like spaghetti. Tristen felt his heart racing.

"He told me this afternoon after we got back from riding," she sobbed. "He doesn't want us to get married. He said his conscience won't let him. I told him I still love him and I still want to marry him, but he said no. He said he wasn't ready."

"Do you want me to talk to him?"

"No. We'll work this out ourselves. Can you just stay here with me for a few minutes?"

"Yeah. I'll stay as long as you want."

Chapter 19

By Friday, Hope had become extremely concerned about Tyla. She usually called or stopped by and Hope hadn't seen or heard from her all week long. When she'd called the hospital, she'd been told that Tyla was off the entire week. Tyla hadn't missed a day of work since she'd started working at Mercy six months ago.

She got Tyla's address off the envelope that contained the get-well card she'd sent her and looked up MapQuest.com driving directions to her house. She'd thought about asking Tristen about Tyla when he came over on Sunday to see Brandon, but two days was too long to wait.

Hope admired the huge log ranch-style home as she pulled into the driveway a little after six behind Tyla's little Volkswagen. There was also a sleek black Rodeo in the driveway.

When she rang the doorbell, she was surprised when Tristen opened the door.

Hope suddenly felt nervous. She rubbed her hands together in front of her. "I'm sorry to just barge in. I've been calling Tyla all week at the hospital. They said she was on leave. I was worried about her and just came by to check on her. Is she okay?"

Tristen didn't know whether or not to share his sister's grief with Hope, although she was bound to find out sooner or later. Hope followed him into the living room.

"She's feeling a little under the weather." A *little* was an understatement for Tyla hadn't come out of her room all week long. "Have a seat. I'll go see if she feels like visiting." Tristen felt confident that his sister would come out of her room to visit Hope.

About a minute later, he returned and attempted a smile. "I'm sorry. She doesn't feel up to visiting at the moment, but you can stay, if you like. Momma's in the kitchen. We were eating supper. You can join us."

Hope stood. "Oh, no, I don't want to be an imposition. I'm sorry I interrupted. I just came to see Tyla."

"It's okay, and you won't be an imposition." He walked toward the kitchen, beckoning her with his hand. "Come on."

Hope followed him into the kitchen. Myah invited Hope to sit down and fixed her a plate of the steamed shrimp and rice and coleslaw she'd just prepared. They chatted while they ate.

Several minutes later, Hope swallowed her last bite of slaw and said, "Myah, thank you. That was delicious."

"You're welcome," Myah said.

Tristen stood. Looking down at Hope, he asked, "Would you like some more?"

"Oh, no, thank you. I'm stuffed."

Tristen took Hope's dishes to the counter, then returned to the table and looked at his mother. "What about you, Momma? Do you want some more or are you finished?"

"Oh, I'm through, dear, but don't worry about the kitchen." She stood. "I'll clean up." She knew how much her eldest son liked Hope because she was all he'd been talking about since last Sunday. "Why don't you keep Hope company?"

His mother would get no arguments from him tonight. Hope followed Tristen out onto the deck into the cool October evening air.

She sucked in a breath of fresh air and surveyed the area. "It's so beautiful here. I could just sit out here forever soaking it all in."

Tristen grinned as he sat back in his chair. "It *is* nice, isn't it? My daddy built this house years ago when we were little."

Hope looked at him curiously. Was he from a broken home, also, like her and her children? "Where's your father now?"

Tristen eyed the golden hues of autumn. "He died several months ago of a heart attack."

Hope's look was sympathetic. "I'm sorry." She felt her heart rate quicken. That could've been her, but she'd been given a second chance. "How old was he?"

"Forty-eight."

Hope shook her head and stated sadly, "So young."

Tristen's tone was quiet. "Yeah." After a brief silence, he said, "Hey, would you like to go see a movie with me?"

"A movie? Now?"

"Yeah. It's Friday and the night is still young."

Anxiety set in. Hope didn't want him getting any wrong ideas. "Tristen, I have to be honest with you. I'm probably old enough to be your mother, but even if I wasn't, I'm not interested in having another relationship."

Tristen eyed her and boldly stated, "I'm thirty. I'll be thirty-one in three months. Momma just turned forty-five last month. Now, I've got enough sense not to ask your age, especially after you've come close to body slamming me on more than one occasion just for talking to you."

Hope couldn't stifle her laugh. "I wasn't gonna body slam you."

"You sure looked and acted like you wanted to. Anyway, you look young and I can't imagine you being a day over thirty-five."

Hope let out a dainty giggle. His compliment had flattered her, but was it just a line to get her to succumb to his invitation to go out with him? She was three years *older* than his mother and he was eighteen years *younger* than her. Nevertheless, age was not a factor as far as her not going out with him. She never wanted to have another relationship or get married again.

Tristen queried, "So is it because I'm younger than you that you won't go out with me?"

Hope shook her head. "No, that has nothing to do with it."

Tristen stared her straight in the eye. "Then what is it? Is it your ex-husband? Did he hurt you so bad that you're scarred for life?"

Hope's solemn reply was, "I guess that's a good way of putting it." She grinned at him. "Now what I'm wondering is why a nice young man like yourself doesn't have a steady girlfriend or a wife."

Tristen sat back and clasped his hands on his chest. "Well, my family says it's because I run away every girl I date because I like things neat and in place."

Hope was impressed. "That's a very unique quality in a man. Most of 'em are slobs."

"Ooh, there's that fire in your eyes again."

Hope's tone turned serious. "There's no fire in my eyes." For some unexplainable reason, she no longer wished to be tough around him.

"Go look at yourself in the mirror. You got one in your pocketbook?" Tristen asked, nodding at her purse. "There's so much fire in your eyes, you could start a forest fire out here. Maybe we better go inside and get away from all these trees. We don't wanna burn up the forest."

Hope found herself willingly laughing again. Suddenly, she was baring a part of herself she didn't talk about with anyone. Why did she feel that she owed him an explanation for her gruffness?

"Look, I can't help how I feel. My husband cheated on me with my best friend. After what they did, it's hard for me to trust anyone, especially men."

"So everybody else has to pay for what your husband and your best friend did to you?"

"I didn't say that."

"But that's how you're acting."

Hope felt herself getting provoked at his retorts. "Listen. I'm the one who suffered through it. I don't appreciate you telling me how I'm supposed to feel and act."

"I wasn't trying to tell you how to feel and act. I just don't understand your reasoning on the situation."

Hope replied despondently, "And you won't until you go through it yourself." She stood. "I better go. Will you ask Tyla to call me when she's up to talking?"

Tristen rose. "You don't have to go on account of me. I didn't mean to make you mad."

"I'm not mad. I really do have to go."

"So I guess your answer to the movie is no?"

"Yes." Hope walked away.

"Wait. I'll show you out."

She called over her shoulder, "It's okay. I remember the way. I'll show myself out."

Myah stepped out onto the deck. "What happened? Hope seemed a little upset when she left."

Tristen eyed his mother. "I may have said some things to her I shouldn't have."

Myah simply turned around and went back inside the house. She wasn't worried so much about Tristen as she was about Tyla at the moment. Now that she was getting older, she was learning that she couldn't fix all her children's problems although she wished she could. Dilemmas like broken toys and scraped knees when they were younger had been a whole lot easier to fix than the grown-up problems they were having now.

Chapter 20

Hope was so glad to be back at work. When she'd arrived, she'd greeted everyone with a smile and they all extended warm wishes to her. She was also happy to see that Tyla was back.

On her way to her workstation, she stopped by Tyla's desk. "How are you?"

Tyla smiled, but Hope noticed that her expression was different. Hope saw a sadness behind Tyla's deep brown eyes.

"Okay. Momma and Tristen told me you stopped by to see me Friday afternoon. Thanks. I really appreciate it. I'm sorry I didn't feel like visiting."

Hope smiled. "You're welcome. It's okay. I understand," she lied. She had no understanding of what Tyla was or had been going through because she still didn't know what had transpired, but she wanted to understand. "I was worried about you. When I called you here, they said you were on leave all week." She leaned her head sideways a little and looked at Tyla inquisitively. "Are you sure you're okay? You just don't seem like yourself."

"I'm fine." Tyla wondered momentarily if her mother or brother had shared with Hope the unhappy details about her relationship with Jon.

"Okay," Hope said doubtfully. She turned to walk away but spun back around. "You wanna grab some lunch together today?"

Tyla nodded. "Yeah. Sure."

At lunch, Tyla and Hope decided to eat in the hospital cafeteria, as Tyla wasn't in the mood to venture out.

Hope was beginning to appreciate how Tyla always said a blessing for her food before she ate it.

When Tyla was done uttering her prayer, Hope tried to make friendly conversation. "I really enjoyed your shower. Just two more weeks before the big day, huh?"

Immediately, tears began to stream down Tyla's face. Well, at least now she had the answer to her earlier curiosity regarding whether or not her mother or Tristen had informed Hope about her and Jon's breakup.

Hope asked, "What's the matter?" and pulled a handful of napkins from the dispenser on the table and handed them to Tyla. "Did I say something wrong?"

Tyla wiped her tears with the napkins and sniffed as she spoke. "There's not going to be a wedding."

Hope's mouth flew open. "Why not? What happened?"

"Jon called it off."

"What? Why?"

Since they were sitting by themselves in a corner of the cafeteria, Tyla sadly related, "He told me he slept with one of his coworkers. I told him I still wanted us to get married, that I still love him, but he said no."

Hope had been about to express her sympathy until Tyla had thrown in that last part about still wanting to marry the creep. "You what? You told him you still wanted to marry him? After what he did to you? Why? Are you crazy?"

Tyla looked at Hope strangely. "Because I love him. We've been friends all my life and I didn't want to lose him."

Hope stared back at Tyla. "For God's sake, Tyla, he cheated on you," she almost screamed.

"I know what he did," Tyla snapped back. She stood up. "Look. I don't need to hear this. I've been through enough already. I can't help how I feel."

Heads started turning in their direction.

Hope said, "I'm sorry. Sit back down. I guess I got a little carried away. I didn't mean to." The last thing she wanted to do was hurt Tyla. She was already feeling Tyla's pain as though it were happening to her all over again. Actually, Jon was the one she was angry at. *Men! You can't trust any of 'em!*

Tyla sat back down but barely touched her food. Hope tried to turn the conversation to something positive, like Tristen's mentoring Brandon. She felt a little guilty for getting angry at Tristen Friday evening and walking out on him.

"Tristen took Brandon horseback riding yesterday. That's the first time Brandon had ever been on a horse."

Tyla attempted to smile and asked, "Did he like it?"

"Yes, he loved it. I think he likes riding a horse now better than he does driving."

Tyla thought back to her own childhood. "Daddy taught all of us to ride when we were real young. I love it, too. We all do."

Hope gave Tyla a look packed with empathy. "Tristen told me your father died several months ago of a heart attack. I'm sorry."

Tyla whispered, "Thank you."

"And you saved my life, even after the terrible way I treated you. I probably wouldn't be sitting here right now if it weren't for you."

Tyla relived the day. "When I saw you lying there on that pavement in the parking deck, it scared me nearly to death. I was so nervous that I didn't remember how many rescue breaths and chest compressions I was giving you. The one thing that really stood out in my mind was what my family and I learned in our first aid and CPR classes—if you lose count, don't worry about it, but do something."

Hope genuinely expressed, "Thank you for saving my life."

Tyla's tone was soft. "God's the one who saved your life. He just used me as the instrument for doing so."

Tyla had just given Hope something to ponder.

Chapter 21

Saturday, November 4th, turned out to be a beautiful autumn day much to Tyla's dismay. For the past several days, she had prayed that the heavens would pour rain, hail, thunder and lightning. The gold and crimson colors of fall painted the Tennessee countryside as the sun peeked from behind the clouds. The temperature was a pleasant sixty-two degrees. It was a beautiful day for an outdoor wedding.

Myah found Tyla sitting on the edge of her antique white cottage-style bed. She was disappointed that Tyla still hadn't cleaned up her room. She sat down beside her daughter and placed a gentle arm around her waist. Tyla laid her head against her mother's shoulder.

Myah leaned her head against her daughter's and whispered, "You're gon' be okay, you know?"

Tears streamed down Tyla's cheeks. "When?"

"In time. You're strong, Tyla. You've got the Jefferson

blood running through your veins. When somebody knocks you down, you get right back up. Now finish getting ready so you can go out with your friends and have a good time."

Tyla protested, "I really don't feel like going anywhere."

Just then, Tristen took a chance on getting his head bitten off by his sister when he stuck it inside her room to deliver a message.

As soon as he saw the condition of the room, the first thing that came out of his mouth was, "Good Lord. This place is a mess."

When Tyla shot him a critical look, he changed his tune and said, "Olivia just called and said they'll be here in twenty minutes." As soon as he'd delivered the message, he turned on his heel, almost running for cover from the heat of his sister's disapproving glare.

Myah said, "You need to get out of this house. If you stay here, you'll have too much time to think." Standing, she gently pulled Tyla up off the bed. "Come on."

Tyla reluctantly obeyed.

Myah started to walk away, saying, "Let me know if you need anything." She closed the door behind her.

Tyla's family had been godsends. They'd notified everyone that there would be no wedding and returned all the gifts she'd gotten at her shower. The owner of the bridal shop where Tyla had purchased her dress had even extended a full refund despite her strict no-refund policy after she'd heard how Tyla had gotten duped by Jon.

Although Tyla had wanted to pay for her own gown, Jon had insisted on paying. When Tristen found out she'd mailed the check to him for the full amount, he'd expressed his utter displeasure, but Tyla didn't feel right keeping Jon's money no matter how much he'd hurt her. As for the ring, she'd returned it to Jon with the check for the dress. Tristen had voiced his opinion about that, too. She knew it was because he loved her, but she was still miffed at him for being so critical of Jon.

Since a few of Tyla's friends from high school had already made plans to be at the wedding, they'd gotten her mother to convince Tyla to go out with them. They knew she needed some cheering up and wanted to be there for her.

Looking through her closet, Tyla selected a pair of white spandex bell-bottoms and a strawberry-pink lace spandex top with a white stretch jacket. She decided to wear her hair up.

Myah and Tristen attempted to keep her occupied with cheerful conversation while she waited to be picked up by her friends.

When Tyla had gone, Myah and Tristen looked at each other across the kitchen table.

Tristen said, "You really think she's gonna be okay?"

"In time," Myah replied.

Tristen shook his head in irritation. "I could kill Jon."

His mother gave him a disapproving look. "Tristen, don't say that."

"Well, Momma, what do you expect me to say? It's how I feel. I know you don't want me to feel this way and I don't, either, but I can't help it. You see what he's putting her through. They were getting married soon, but he just couldn't wait. I'll never forgive him for what he did. I could forgive him if he hurt me, but not Tyla, not my sister." Tristen shook his head again.

Myah expressed what her heart was telling her. "Tristen, I believe Jon is having a tougher time forgiving himself than you'll ever have forgiving him."

Tristen shot his mother a stunned look. "Yeah, right," he huffed.

"Think about it. He didn't have to tell Tyla, but he did. He could've just kept his secret and married her anyway. Think about what he's probably going through."

"Momma, how can you sit there and tell me to think about what he's going through? I don't give a flyin' flip about him. Tyla's my concern. It's her I'm thinking about, not him."

The hatred Myah saw in her son's eyes frightened her. It was the kind of look that made a sane person go insane. She reasoned, "Jon has been friends with you boys for a long time."

"That was before he hurt Tyla."

Myah put up her hand. "Let me finish. Tyla's gon' be okay. It's Jon I'm worried about."

Tristen bolted up from his chair. "Momma, how can you say that? He's got his little coworker to keep him happy while—" Tristen waved his hand in the air "—Tyla's out with some of her high school friends trying not to think about the fact that's she's supposed to be marrying him today."

"I know. But, Tristen, remember how Jon always looked up to you boys. You were more like brothers instead of just good friends. Now he's got to live with what he did for the rest of his life."

Tristen started to walk away. "Momma, I'm leaving. I don't want to talk about Jon and his precious feelings anymore."

Myah watched her son walk away. Maybe the news she'd gotten earlier in the week from Jon's parents would cause Tristen to have a change of heart. She yelled after him. "Jon quit his job at the hospital. He transferred to University of Alabama-Birmingham Hospital."

Tristen kept walking. As far as he was concerned, Jon Jenkins could drop off the face of the planet.

Tristen was on his way out the front door when the telephone rang. He was in no mood to talk to anyone so he decided to let his mother answer it. When she hadn't picked up by the third ring, he stepped over to the sofa table and snatched the phone off the hook.

"Hello." He spoke harshly into the receiver.

The female voice on the other end said, "May I speak to Tyla?"

"She's not here." Tristen continued to speak in a not too pleasant tone.

"Aah, what time do you expect her back?"

"I don't know what time she'll be back. Do you wanna leave a message or what?"

"Is this Tristen?"

"Who wants to know?"

"Tristen? Hi, it's Hope."

Tristen's tone quickly became gentler and he allowed his

shoulders to relax. "Hope, I'm sorry. I didn't mean to be so rude."

"It's okay. Are you all right? You sound upset about something. I didn't recognize your voice at first."

He released a heavy sigh. "I'm fine."

"Okay," Hope stated doubtfully. "I was just calling to see if Tyla wanted to go to a movie or something. I mean, I know she was supposed to get married today and I just thought I'd try to do something to cheer her up. How's she doing?"

Tristen walked around the sofa with the cordless phone to his ear and plopped down. "About as well as can be expected, I guess. She's out with some of her high school friends who were planning on being at the wedding. They wanted to take her out, too."

"That's nice." Hope paused. "Are you sure you're okay?"

"I'm fi—" he started to fib again. "No, I'm not okay. I've got a lot on my mind," he stated without the least bit of embarrassment.

Hope surprised herself when she asked, "Would you like to see a movie with me?"

Tristen's mood suddenly turned jovial. "*You're* asking me out? Doesn't that break all your rules about men?"

"It's not a date. Just two friends hanging out."

A broad grin covered Tristen's face. "Oh, so we're friends now?"

Hope plunged into a sea of laughter. "Listen, I'm not going to have a debate with you. Do you wanna go or not?"

"Sure. What time does the movie start?"

Hope checked the times she'd written down on the piece of paper in front of her. "The next one starts at four. It's almost three now. Can you pick me up around three-thirty, or would you like for me to pick you up?"

"No, I don't want you to pick me up," Tristen stated whimsically. "I'll see you at three-thirty."

"Hey, don't you wanna know what we're seeing?"

"I don't care as long you're paying."

"Humph. You wish."

"Well, you invited me." He broke into hearty laughter. "I'm kidding. As long as it's a good, *clean* movie, I'm all for it. Anything objectionable and I'm walking out."

Hope grinned. She liked his attitude.

When they ended the call, Tristen was grinning from ear to ear, too.

After the movie, Hope and Tristen ate dinner at a local restaurant near the theater.

Hope peeked at him as she ate her hickory-stuffed baked potato. "You wanna hit him, don't you?"

Tristen gave her a look filled with confusion. "Do what?"

"I've figured out why you were so grumpy on the phone earlier. I know how protective you and your brothers are of Tyla."

Tristen wondered what his sister had told Hope about him, Torey and Terrell.

"You wanna hit him. What's his name?"

Tristen shifted in his seat. "Jon."

"You wanna open up a can of whip tail on him for what

he did to Tyla, don't you? I know I wouldn't mind getting a good whack at him myself."

"Well, I'm warning you, don't do it. Seems like you and she are becoming friends. I'm not saying it didn't cross my mind, but it wouldn't be right. Our parents raised us better than that."

Hope shook her head. "I have to tell you that I've never met anyone quite like your family."

Tristen gave her a questioning gaze. "What d'you mean?"

"Well, first, Tyla told me she still wanted to marry the creep even after he told her what he did and now you're talking about what's morally right. I respect y'all's warm and fuzzy feelings for the guy, but I just don't understand how you can be so forgiving of someone who hurt you or your family like that. I've come to the conclusion that there's only one explanation for it."

Tristen was eager to hear what she had to say. "What's that?"

Hope quickly stated, "You're all just plain weird."

He chuckled.

Hope went on. "I'm just saying I've never met anyone like your family before."

"We're not saints by any means, but our parents raised us to treat people with dignity and respect. To treat them the way we want to be treated—you know, the Golden Rule."

"Yeah, I used to believe in that Golden-Rule stuff and look at what it got me. A husband sleeping around with my best friend."

Tristen cut his eyes at her. "Are you going to be bitter about it for the rest of your life?"

"I don't know. Maybe. How long are you going to be mad at your friend for what he did to your sister?"

As Tristen thought about it, he could still feel the resentment and hostility brewing in his belly.

Chapter 22

Tristen studied Hope's face. "You're a tough cookie, aren't you?"

Hope set down her water glass. "That's what happens when you get burned."

"You're afraid of getting hurt again," Tristen brazenly stated. "I'll tell you what I think."

She forced herself to wait to hear his viewpoint even though she wasn't sure she wanted to.

Tristen kept his eyes glued to hers. "I think you're like those little M&M candies. You're hard on the surface, but inside, you're all soft."

Hope didn't know whether to be pleased or offended at his statement. "What makes you say that?"

"Well, it's a known fact that when some people get hurt, they go into a kind of defense mode with everybody in order to keep from getting hurt again. And I can understand that. But

I've seen how you are with your children—so warm and loving."

Hope threw back her head and said, "Ha! You have to be that way with your kids."

"Yeah, but not all parents are. I see it every day. Some of the kids we work with have committed some horrific crimes. But then, there are others with less severe offenses. Yet some of them have very little, if any, family support. But look at you, you're trying to raise your kids right and you're trying to be there for them."

Hope lowered her eyes. "I'm just doing what any mother would do."

"*Most* mothers," he kindly reminded her.

She didn't want to talk about herself anymore. "Brandon really likes you. I appreciate your taking out some of your time to spend with him. The divorce hasn't been easy on any of us but especially not for him. You know, a boy needs his father."

Hope glanced at Tristen and he gave her an understanding nod. "Even though he's behind in his child-support payments, I still let Lance see the kids. They need that."

Tristen flicked a piece of white lint off the burgundy tablecloth. It was his fourth or fifth time tonight doing it. Hope could see that he was somewhat of a perfectionist, but she didn't find it the least bit unappealing. As she'd told him, it was a very rare trait in a man. She attempted to refocus on their conversation.

Tristen warmly commented, "That's very admirable. Despite your bitter feelings for your ex-husband, you don't allow them to distance him from his children."

Hope was quick to say, "Well, I do it for the kids, certainly not for him."

Hope and Tristen had been so engrossed in their conversation that the time had quickly slipped away from them. It was nearly eleven o'clock.

Tristen commented, "Time sure flies when you're having fun."

Hope felt pleased that he considered talking to her fun. Much to her surprise, she'd thoroughly enjoyed being with him, too.

Tristen paid their waitress before they exited the restaurant. They talked some more on the drive to Hope's apartment. When they arrived, she told him what a nice time she'd had. He offered to walk her to her door, but she insisted on going alone. She didn't want him to get the wrong idea about them; she was truly beginning to like him, but only as a friend. She liked that he waited in his car until she was safely inside her apartment. He was such a caring individual.

The last time Myah had been this nervous about her only daughter coming home from a night out was the day Tyla had gone on her first date when she was sixteen. Now she was a grown woman out with a few of her girlfriends, but Myah was just as anxious as she had been that day. Tyla was at a very vulnerable stage of her life. There was no telling how long it would take her to get completely over her and Jon's breakup.

Myah was still in her bedroom rummaging through a

trunk full of memorabilia from the kids' childhood years when Tyla got home a little after midnight. Tyla stopped in the doorway and peeked inside.

"Hey, Momma. You still up?"

Myah turned slightly from her spot on the floor in front of the trunk and smiled easily. "Hey, baby. Yeah. I couldn't sleep."

Tyla walked toward her mother. "Why not? Were you worried about me? You don't have to be, you know. I'm feeling a lot better."

Myah brushed her shoulder up against Tyla's leg. "You're my baby. I can't help it." Looking up into her daughter's face, she inquired, "Did you have a good time?"

Tyla took off her high heels, dropped them onto the carpet, and sat cross-legged on the floor beside her mother. "Yes, it was fun. Whatcha doing?"

Myah turned her attention back to her trunk of goodies. "Oh, just rummaging through some of the things you kids made when you were young." Pulling out a colorful Crayola picture, she passed it to Tyla. "Remember this?"

Tyla took the drawing and surveyed it with steady eyes. "Yes. Your Mother's Day card, I made it for you when I was in first grade."

The entire family always teased Myah about being such a pack rat. Now, Tyla was glad for it. She loved looking through the drawings and crafts she'd made when she was young. "Momma, you keep everything."

"Everything that means something to me. I've still got y'all's report cards in here and old newspaper clippings from when you made honor roll and joined the summer reading program at the library."

Tyla's smile added extra light and warmth to the room. "That's so sweet."

They looked at several more pieces of artwork that Tyla and her brothers had made before Tyla kissed her mother's cheek and rose to call it a night. She grabbed her shoes.

Looking down at her mother, she said, "This was really special, Momma—going through these things with you. It brought back some really fond memories. Good night." Tyla turned and sauntered toward the door.

Without looking up, Myah uttered, "Did you know Jon quit his job at the hospital? He transferred to Birmingham."

Tyla stopped in the doorway. "No, I didn't know. When? Who told you?"

Myah looked at Tyla this time. "He moved a couple of weeks ago. His mother called me last night and told me. His family feels really bad about what happened, as he does. You know they've always adored you."

Tyla couldn't believe that Jon had left without uttering a word of his departure to her or saying goodbye. But then again, what did she expect? Nevertheless, they'd been lifelong friends. It just didn't seem right that he was gone. There was no telling when or if she'd see him again.

Myah stood. "Are you okay?"

The partial joy she'd felt from her evening out with her friends had suddenly melted away. Tyla would not try to pretend with her mother. She shook her head. "No. I can't believe he's gone. He didn't even say goodbye."

Myah stared at her daughter's back. As much as she'd hated to give Tyla the news about Jon, she'd known that she had to. "Honey, that was the old Jon who wouldn't have gone without saying goodbye. He's a different person now."

Hot tears slipped down Tyla's cheeks. "No matter what happened between us, I still care about him. I still love him. I wish he could have seen that so we could have gone ahead with the wedding. He didn't have to leave."

Myah went to Tyla. Placing her hands on her arms, she slowly turned her daughter to face her and slid her thumbs underneath her wet eyes to wipe away the tears. "I think deep down inside, he knows you still love him. Maybe he's having a hard time loving himself right now."

Myah wrapped her arms around Tyla until she was ready to be released. One of Tyla's best friends was gone. No more would they go riding together on his motorcycle, horseback riding, fishing or anything else. Even a simple phone conversation seemed unattainable now.

After church, Tyla caught up with Tristen in the church parking lot as he made his way to his vehicle.

She yelled, "Hey, why you in such a rush? You can't speak to your own family?"

Tristen turned around, grinning from ear to ear. He walked toward his sister and threw his arms around her. "Hey, sis."

"Hey." Tyla's expression suddenly turned melancholy. "Did Momma tell you Jon moved to Alabama?"

The smile disappeared from Tristen's face. At least she didn't appear devastated. "Yeah."

"Tristen, please don't hate him," his sister begged. "If I can get over what he did, why can't you? I mean, it happened to me, not you."

"You're my little sister. It's my job to pro—"

"I'm not your little sister anymore. I'm your *grown* sister and it's my job to protect myself. You and Jon, all of us, have been friends for a long time. Don't let this one little incident mess that up."

"It's not a *little* incident. And he's the one who messed up everything. Why are you defending him? Aren't you the least bit angry?"

"Yes, I'm hurt and angry. But like I said, I still love him."

"Hope was right," Tristen mumbled. "Our family is weird."

Tyla's eyes lit up. "Hope? When'd you talk to her?"

"Last night when you were out. She called to see if you wanted to go see a movie with her. She knew you were probably feeling down. But you weren't in and she and I went out instead."

Tyla grinned broadly. "So did you have a good time?"

Tristen's smile returned. "Yes."

Tyla took her brother's hands in hers. "So tell me about it."

"There's nothing to tell. We went to see a movie, then went to eat. We sat at the restaurant for hours just talking. Then I took her home."

Tyla grinned some more as she leaned back on her heels. "You didn't try to kiss her good-night, did you?"

Tristen joked, "Excuse you. You're being a little nosy, aren't you?"

"I just hope you didn't try to kiss her on the first date. That's a major no-no." Tyla shook a finger at him. "Most women don't like to be kissed the first time they go out with a guy."

"Ah, excuse me. I'm thirty years old to your twenty-two. I think I know the dos and don'ts of dating."

Tyla relaxed a bit and spoke with certainty. "No, you didn't try to kiss her."

"And how do you know if I did or not?"

Tyla surveyed his face meticulously. "Well, I don't see any black eyes. And I'm sure Hope would've socked you if you'd tried."

They were laughing when their mother approached them.

Tyla said excitedly, "Momma, did you know Tristen took Hope out last night?"

Tristen gave his sister a playful evil eye. "Big mouth."

Myah grabbed their hands in hers. "No, he didn't tell me. So how was it?"

Tristen laughed again. "How was it? Y'all are acting like it's been eons since I've been out with a woman."

Tyla teased, "Well, it *has* been a while."

They laughed as Tristen gave his sister a playful warning. "You better watch it." Then he added, "For your information, we're going out again today."

Tyla squealed with excitement.

Tristen said, "Dawg, Tyla. Why don't you just call the *Guiness Book of World Records?*"

Chapter 23

Despite her desire to only be friends with Tristen, Hope was really looking forward to going out with him again today. He was taking her horseback riding, a feat she'd never before tackled. She mentally chastised herself for acting like a giddy teenager as she awaited his arrival.

Tristen couldn't wait to see Hope again. He liked spending time with her and talking with her despite some of her narrow-minded views and he tried to keep in mind that she was a woman scorned. She had said that she just wanted to be friends, but he could tell that she really liked him, too. As much as she tried to make him believe she hated all men, it hadn't taken long for her icy coating to melt away.

Tristen picked up Hope and drove to the ranch. She was a little frightened of the horses at first so he suggested she ride with him. Afterward, he walked alongside the horse while she rode. Only then had she gained the courage to attempt a ride by herself.

On the drive to a nearby restaurant to get dinner, Hope expressed how much fun she'd had.

She said gleefully, "Tyla said your father taught ya'll to ride when you were real young."

"Yes. Momma and Daddy met at a rodeo when I was still a baby."

Hope wrinkled her eyebrows. "They met when you were a baby?"

"Yeah. I don't have the same father as Tyla and my brothers. My stepfather married my mom when I was two and he adopted me. I don't know my real father. He walked off on Momma when he found out she was pregnant."

Hope looked tenderly at Tristen. "Oh, that's horrible."

Tristen showed no trace of sorrow or regret. "It's okay. My father treated me just like I was his own. There was never any half this or that in our family. To us, I was just as much a whole part of them as everyone else was."

Hope smiled. "That's nice."

Tristen glanced her way briefly. "What about your family?"

Hope's tone seemed to turn sour. "I have a younger sister and two older brothers. Our parents divorced when we were young. Both of them died several years ago. My siblings and I don't keep in contact with each other. I don't even know where they live and as far as I know, they don't know where I live, either. We were never very close and the divorce just made it worse." That was one of the reasons she liked Tristen's family so much—they seemed to have such a strong family bond. She had endeavored for her children to have what she hadn't had with her own family.

Tristen looked at Hope. "Well, I can tell you from experience that it's not always flesh and blood that makes a family but the love you give and get in return from the people in your life, no matter who they are."

Tristen had such a positive attitude despite the fact that his biological father had abandoned him, and he'd never gotten an opportunity to know him. Yet, every time she was around him, Hope felt nothing but sheer joy reverberating from him.

When Tristen pulled his Rodeo up into a parking space in front of Hope's apartment, Brandon and his sisters had just gotten out of a vehicle a couple of spaces over. He and Hope went to greet the teenagers. While Ashlee and Brittney headed toward the apartment, Tristen stood on the sidewalk talking with Brandon. He noticed that Hope had walked over to the car her teenagers had gotten out of and was conversing with the male driver. Hope had just given Lance another stern reminder about his late child-support payments.

Ignoring her, Lance frowned and abruptly asked, "Who's that dude?" He knew who the guy was because he'd been all their son talked about lately and he wasn't happy that another man was trying to take over his role as father to his children. He only asked Hope the question to put her on the spot and see what her response would be.

Hope refused to turn around and look at Tristen for fear that he would see her and know that he was the topic of her and Lance's conversation.

She answered nonchalantly, "That's Tristen Jefferson, my coworker's brother. He's a juvenile probation officer," she added, thinking that might shut her ex's mouth.

"What's he doing? Making home visits on a Sunday? Brandon's not being supervised by the juvenile authorities anymore and this guy wasn't even his caseworker. Brandon had a woman officer. What's this guy doing here?"

Hope suddenly grew hot with anger. She attempted to whisper. "It's none of your business what he's doing here. You know, you've got a lot of nerve coming over here asking insinuating questions."

"It is my business. Brandon's my son." With a short laugh, Lance added, "And they're not insinuating questions unless you tryin' to hide something. Are you?" he asked, peering at her.

Hope steadied herself. "Unfortunately, you're right— Brandon is your business. But *I'm* not."

"Oh, so is this guy your new beau? Looks a little too young for you, if you ask me. How old is he? Twenty? You robbin' the cradle, ain't cha?" Lance heckled.

"You don't worry about how old he is. Just go."

Lance laughed again. "Why you gettin' mad? I just asked a question."

Hope yelled, "You dropped off the kids! Now will you just leave?"

Suddenly, Tristen was at her side. "Are you okay?"

Lance said, "Everything's fine, pal. My wife and I were just talkin'."

Hope firmly stated, "Your *ex*-wife."

Tristen reached his hand out toward Lance. "Hi, I'm Tris—"

Before he could get the rest out, Lance had backed his car out of the space and had taken off out of the complex. Brandon joined his mother and Tristen.

Hope fumed, "Now you can see why I divorced his butt." She felt instant regret. As much as she despised Lance, she tried not to speak negatively of him around the children, but he had made her so angry that she'd said the first thing that had come to her mind.

Tristen asked again, "Are you okay?"

"I'll be fine."

Tristen looked at Brandon and said, "Take your mother inside. See you Friday." He had made plans to take Brandon to the high school football game Friday.

Brandon said, "Okay. See ya." He and his mother made their way toward their apartment.

Hope wanted to look back at Tristen and see him one last time before he left, but she willed herself to keep her eyes focused straight ahead.

Chapter 24

The next morning when they had registered all their waiting patients, Hope entered Tyla's cubicle.

She whispered, "Hey, did you hear about the layoffs?"

Tyla looked curiously at her coworker. "What layoffs?"

Hope leaned down. "Here at the hospital. I heard there's going to be some major layoffs."

"Maybe it's just a rumor."

"I hope that's all it is. I can't afford to lose my job."

"Even if it's true, surely they'll go by seniority. You've been here three years, haven't you?"

"Almost, but some have been here a lot longer than that."

"Well, I wouldn't worry too much about it if I were you. God will provide."

Hope asked sarcastically, "Is God going to drop a job in my lap or make food miraculously appear on my table and put clothes on my and my kids' backs?"

Tyla gave Hope a stern look of disapproval. "As long as we put him first in our lives, he'll make sure we have what we need. That's what the Bible says at Matthew, chapter six, verses twenty-five through thirty-four. He takes care of the animals and clothes the vegetation of the field. Therefore, he'll provide for us, his human creation."

Hope had never heard Tyla speak so brazenly about her faith. She respected it, but she couldn't wait around for God to make things happen for her and her family. She didn't want to hear any more and decided to make her exit.

"Well, I'll talk to you later. I better get back to my desk. They're probably watching us like hawks now and'll be using any little excuse to get rid of us."

Hope went back to her station and Tyla refocused her attention on her computer screen.

Later that afternoon when Tyla and Tristen went riding, Tyla shared with her brother what Hope had told her.

Tyla said, "She's really worried about losing her job."

Tristen responded, "That's understandable. After all, she's a single parent with three teenagers to take care of."

Tyla adjusted the reins in her hands. "I tried to tell her that God will provide what her family needs, but she didn't seem to want to hear it."

"Maybe that's because she has no hope or trust in him because of what she's been through."

Tyla looked thoughtful. "Maybe."

Tyla couldn't imagine what it would be like to not have any hope whatsoever about one's life and future. If she hadn't any, there would be no way she could cope with the challenges of her faith. Perhaps Hope just needed a little help to find her way back to hers.

Hope was stunned when she opened the door and saw Lance. He asked her to step outside so he could speak with her and wasted no time in voicing his complaints.

"I think you're setting a bad example for the kids with that young dude you're seeing."

Hope couldn't believe his nerve. She was only interested in Tristen as a friend, but Lance's cutthroat inference had just rubbed her the wrong way. "That sure is the pot calling the kettle black, don't you think?"

"What are you talking about?"

"What am I talking about?" Hope echoed. "How about you and Leeza?"

"Well, ah, that was different."

"Oh, was it? How so?"

"Well, she's not half my age and we weren't doing anything around the kids."

Hope folded her arms. She decided to disregard his comments about Tristen's age. She mocked him. "At least you were discreet when you cheated on me."

Lance took in a deep breath of air and released it. "Hope, that's in the past and I've told you a thousand times I'm sorry."

"So that's supposed to make it better. You think you can kiss the boo-boo and make it go away?"

"That guy's too young for you and you know it," Lance snapped. "He looks like he could be the kids' brother. What if Brandon or Ashlee or Brittney for that matter, dated someone way younger than them?"

Hope yelled, "Brandon, Ashlee and Brittney are teenagers, and Ashlee and Brittney aren't even allowed to date yet. When they become adults, they can do what they want." She threw up her hand and turned to walk away. "I'm through talking about this. You don't run my life. Go home to your wife."

Lance quickly caught up with her. "I don't want him around my kids. You better stop seeing him or I'll have you in court for full custody so fast, you'll feel your head spin."

Hope stopped dead in her tracks and turned on him. "Don't you threaten me. I've put up with you being behind in child-support payments ever since we divorced almost three years ago, but never once have I tried to keep you from seeing the kids. So you better back your butt up off of me. There's talk of layoffs at the hospital.

"As much as I hate to have to ask you for anything more, not that I'll get it, you better be prepared to contribute more toward your children's needs, just in case. I'm the one who's working both a full- and a part-time job—killing myself trying to take care of our children," she reminded him. "So if anybody gets taken back to court, buddy, it'll be you. Now get outta my face."

With that said, Hope turned on her heel and returned to her apartment.

By Friday, word had spread rapidly around the hospital about possible layoffs. At lunch, Hope told Tyla about Lance's visit earlier in the week.

Tyla commented, "It sounds like he's jealous."

Hope looked at Tyla. "Tristen and I are just friends."

"Did you tell Lance that?"

Hope was hesitant. "Well, not exactly."

"What d'you mean, not exactly?"

"He made me so mad, I just let him think what he wanted to."

Tyla lowered her eyes to the food on her plate. "Hope, I don't know whether or not you're aware of it, but Tristen really does like you. Please don't string him along. If you only want to be friends, tell him that."

Hope gave Tyla a forlorn look. "I've told him. Believe me, after what people have done to me, I pride myself on being honest and up-front about my feelings. I really do like him, too, but just as a dear friend. At this point in my life, I don't want another relationship. I've told him that, too."

"Then why do you keep going out with him every time he asks you to?"

"Tyla, we're just friends. It's just two friends hanging out."

"Not to him."

"So what do you suggest? That I stop seeing him?"

"I'm not suggesting anything. I'm just telling you how he feels about you. I don't want him to get hurt. He's too nice a person to be strung along."

Hope gave Tyla a disapproving glare. "I'm both shocked and offended that you would insinuate that I'm stringing him alone. I care about him. I would never intentionally hurt him. I know I'm not the nicest person in the world, but I know firsthand what it's like to be betrayed and I would never do that to anyone."

"I'm not saying you would. But remember, he was my brother first, before he ever knew you, and I care about him a whole lot more than you do."

Hope didn't know what to do. She had been struggling to fight her growing feelings toward Tristen and had told herself over and over that she could keep them under control. But who did she think she was fooling?

Chapter 25

Nearly two weeks later, Thanksgiving rolled around. Upon Myah's invitation, Hope spent the holiday at the Jeffersons'. Her children were with Lance for the remainder of the week. Hope loved the Jefferson family. They always made her and the children feel as though they were family.

After dinner, everyone sat around talking and sharing laughs. When Tristen excused himself for a moment, Myah noticed the look of adoration in Hope's eyes as she watched him disappear.

"You like him, don't you?"

"Excuse me?" Hope said.

Myah grinned. "Tristen. You like him. Don't you?"

Hope found herself blushing and gave a nervous laugh. "Yes, but I don't feel comfortable talking to you about it."

"Why not?"

"Because you're his mother."

"And?"

Hope cast a glance Myah's way. "It wouldn't bother you for an older woman like me to date your son?" She was quick to add, "I'm not saying that I'm going to because I'm still suffering some emotional pain from my first marriage. I'm just asking."

Myah didn't want to pry, but thought it necessary that Hope know of her deep concern for her. "Your ex-husband hurt you pretty bad, huh?"

Hope blinked. "Yes. My best friend, too. They had an affair."

Myah flinched from the empathy she felt in her heart for Hope. "Whew. That must've been a really tough pill to swallow."

Hope's eyes began to glisten with tears. "It was."

Myah attempted to redirect the conversation. "To answer your question about whether or not it would bother me for an older woman to date my son—no, it wouldn't. But then again, it doesn't matter what I think because Tristen's a grown man." She added comically, "Even though he does act like a teenager at times."

To her surprise, Hope found herself defending him. "He's young at heart, but he's very responsible. He's been a good role model for Brandon. Brandon really looks forward to seeing him every week."

Myah grinned. "Not to brag, but everybody likes Tristen. From the day he was born, I knew he'd be special in his own way. Even then, he was his own person. He's never been one to go along with the crowd, simply for the sake of blending in with everybody else. When he turned two, though, I wanted to throw him away. He's the only one of my kids who went through that terrible-two stage. Did your kids go through that?" She looked at Hope.

Hope rubbed her temple. "I don't remember."

Myah exclaimed, "They must not have. If they had, believe me, you'd remember."

Hope broke into a wide smile.

Myah continued, "He'd pitch a tantrum in a heartbeat. I remember one Sunday when we were at church, he got mad at me about something. He grabbed that songbook outta my hand and threw it clear across the room. When he saw the crazed look in my eyes, he knew he was fixin' to be spanked. Before I could get ahold of him, he started yelling at the top of his lungs, 'Oh, God, help me. Please help me, Lord.'"

Hope burst into laughter.

Myah went on, "There was this little girl sitting beside us who was a little older than him—probably four. She looked at Tristen and said, 'The Lord ain't gon' help you.'"

Hope was rolling over with laughter. "No, she didn't."

"Yes, she did. I yanked him up, marched him to the restroom, and tore his li'l hiney up."

Myah and Hope were dying laughing.

Tristen returned, catching the tail end of his mother's story. "Momma, don't be telling my business now."

Hope smiled as Tristen rejoined her on the living room sofa. "Aw, now. She was just sharing some of your childhood stories with me."

Myah said, "Lord, am I glad he got all that badness out of his system back then. Otherwise, he wouldn't have made it to thirty."

Myah's heart melted at the sound of Tristen and Hope's deep laughter.

"I really like your family," Hope told Tristen later that afternoon as they sat on the swing in the Jeffersons' backyard.

Tristen grinned proudly. "They like you and your kids, too."

"Well, my kids certainly like them a lot."

Tristen leaned in a little closer and whispered, "I'll tell you something else, too."

"What?" Hope asked in a soft, low tone.

"I sure do like their mother a lot."

Hope grew nervous and tried to inch away as she let out a little giggle. "That's sweet."

Tristen countered, "I'm not trying to be sweet. I'm serious. I've never felt about a woman the way I feel about you, Hope."

"Ah, Tristen, I told you I just want us to be friends."

"Are you sure that's all you want? I know you like me, too."

She wondered for a brief moment if he'd overheard the entire conversation earlier between her and his mother.

Tristen went on, "When we first met, you were a tigress. You acted like you wanted to scratch my eyeballs out. Now you're this lovable little pussycat. You say you just want to be friends, but I think your heart is telling you something else."

He was so close to her now that Hope could feel his sweet, warm breath on her neck. When she attempted to inch over some more, she realized she couldn't move any farther.

She let out a fake chuckle. "Tristen, I—"

Before Hope realized what had happened, Tristen had covered her mouth with his. His lips were soft. The gray matter inside her head kept urging her to resist him, but her heart kept demanding that it shut up. After several seconds, the kiss ended. She felt as though she were floating on a cloud. When she opened her eyes and came to her senses, she jumped off the swing.

"You shouldn't have done that," Hope firmly stated.

Tristen stood and broke into a huge grin. "I didn't hear any complaints when I was doing it."

"That's not funny," she protested.

"Didn't you like it?"

Hope began to look around her, anywhere but at him.

Tristen lifted his hand to her chin and turned her face toward his. "Did you like it?"

Hope started to walk away. "It doesn't matter whether I liked it or not. You shouldn't have done it. We're in your family's yard where anybody can see us. What if my kids were here? It's this kind of behavior that gets people into trouble—the kind that leads them to do other things."

Tristen followed her and stood in her path. "Hope, all I did was kiss you. Whether we're at your place or mine, alone or in a crowded room, I would never try to get you to do anything more."

Hope looked down at the ground. "You never know

what'll happen in the heat of the moment." Why was she feeling like some scared little teenager?

Against his will, Tristen thought about Jon. "You're right. I guess I wasn't thinking clearly because I like you so much."

"Will you take me home, please?"

He tenderly took her wrists in his hands. "Why so early? It's only four o'clock. It's because I kissed you, isn't it?"

"No," she truthfully answered. She didn't want to leave because he'd kissed her, but rather, because she felt herself falling in love with him. "I'm not feeling good. I just wanna go home and lie down."

Tristen held his hand out toward the house. "Well, you can lie down here. Momma won't mind. She's got five bedrooms. You can take your pick."

Hope shook her head. "No, no. I prefer to lie in my own bed."

"Okay. I'll take you then. Let's go." He held out his hand to her.

She didn't think it was wise to take his hand, but Hope didn't want to hurt his feelings. Initially, she hesitated but they walked hand in hand back toward the house. Hope got her purse and bid everyone farewell while Myah fixed her a to-go plate.

On the drive to her apartment, Hope was quiet as her thoughts kept whirling around in her head. *You big dummy. Whatever made you think you could just be friends with the guy and not fall in love with him? You're not a child. You're a grown woman. You're almost forty-nine years old. You should've known better.*

Tristen attempted to make light conversation along

the way, but Hope only responded every now and then. What had she gotten herself into?

For the next two days, Tristen telephoned Hope and she refused to answer his calls. He left several messages, but she didn't return any of them. Around midmorning, she heard someone knocking on the door.

She heard Tristen saying, "Hope, I know you're in there. Please open the door. Why are you avoiding me? Are you okay?"

After his pleas continued to go unanswered, he finally left. Hope sure hoped her neighbors hadn't witnessed him banging on her door. The last thing she needed was people gossiping about them.

She was putting in as many hours as she could at the Junction while the kids were with their father. Today, she was working second shift, but by the time her shift started at three, she was so worked up that it was difficult for her to concentrate as she rang up customers' purchases. All she could think about was Tristen and the pickle she'd gotten herself into. She had been determined never to fall in love again, but she'd done exactly the opposite. She could kick herself. How had she let this happen? She was too old for this. It wasn't that Tristen wasn't a great guy. He was terrific, but then, hadn't Lance been, also, before he'd started messing around with Leeza? She had to stop seeing Tristen. She couldn't take a chance at being hurt again.

At about six-thirty, Hope got a shock when she saw that Tristen was her next customer in line, with many others behind him. Her heart began to pump ten times faster than normal.

She attempted to greet him with a smile. "Hi."

"Hello. Why haven't you returned my calls?" Tristen was trying to be discreet. "Or answer the door when I came by this morning." He lacked his usual cheerfulness.

"I haven't been feeling well," she responded as she bagged his items.

He probed, "What's the matter? Are you sick? Do you need to go to the doctor? You know, you need to take better care of yourself."

"No. Just some emotional stuff."

"What time do you get your break?"

She was trying to bag his items quickly so he wouldn't have a reason to prolong his visit. "Seven."

Tristen checked his watch. "It's six-thirty. We need to talk. I'm gonna take my things home and meet you back at the McDonald's here inside the store. If I'm a few minutes late, wait for me."

Hope gave him his change and receipt. "Tristen, don't do this." She tried to speak in a low whisper so no one else would hear.

He looked her square in the eyes and firmly stated, "I'll see you at seven or shortly thereafter." Then he was gone.

Chapter 26

Hope had gotten held up by about five minutes ringing up the last customer in her line before her break. When she arrived at McDonald's at nine minutes after seven, she spotted Tristen sitting at a table in the back corner. He saw her and waved as she stood in line to order her food.

She slowly made her way toward him as though she were walking a death march. She set her tray onto the table and joined him.

"Why are you avoiding me?" he asked.

Hope propped an elbow onto the table and placed her fingers across her forehead. She looked down at her food when she spoke. "Tristen, I told you from the beginning that I don't want to be in a relationship. I only want to be your friend."

Tristen eyed her. "If you only want to be my friend, why'd you kiss me back when I kissed you?"

Hope decided to be honest with him. Perhaps he'd be more accepting of her feelings. "I kissed you because I really and truly do like you, but like I told you, I don't want a relationship. I should have resisted, but I just couldn't at the time. Lance put me through hell with his deceit—with my best friend, of all people. I can't take a chance on going through that again."

Tristen's reply was laced with sincerity. "Hope, when are you going to stop making yourself and everybody else pay for what Lance and your best friend did to you? Don't you deserve to be happy? Don't you *want* to be happy? Life is full of chances. Otherwise, we'd never get anywhere. Is that really it, or is it because of my age? I don't care that I'm younger than you. I'm a grown man. You're a grown woman. We deserve to be together if that's what we both want."

"Your age has nothing to do with it. I don't want to be involved in another relationship, period. I'm sorry if I led you on. I thought we could just be friends. I didn't know I was going to fall—" She refused to say the rest.

A ray of hope tumbled across Tristen's heart and he finished the sentence for her. "In love with me. Why do you want to fight it? Why don't you just let it happen?"

"I don't *want* to fight it, but I *have* to."

Tristen used the next several minutes while they ate to try to persuade Hope to let her feelings flow.

At seven twenty-five, she looked at her watch and said, "I can't. We can only be friends." Then she stood, grabbed her tray and rushed away.

Tristen called out, "Can I still see Brandon?"

Hope turned around and a smile crossed her lips. "Sure. I think he'll like that."

"What's wrong with you?" Tyla asked Tristen the next day after morning worship service. "You're acting and sounding all dry."

Tristen didn't want to discuss his personal business in church for all to hear. "You feel up to a ride later this afternoon?"

"Yeah, sure. What time?"

"Three o'clock?"

"Sure. See ya then."

Tristen walked away right before their mother approached.

Myah asked, "Is Tristen okay? He's been in the best mood all week. Now, all of a sudden, he seems so gloomy."

"I don't know. He wants me to go riding with him this afternoon. I guess I'll find out then."

Tristen felt kind of odd confiding in his baby sister about him and Hope, but on the way to the ranch, he gave Tyla the latest update.

Tyla's heart went out to her older brother. "You want me to talk to her?"

Tristen made a face. "No, I don't want you to talk to her. I don't need my baby sister doing my talking. I was just telling you what happened."

Tyla's tone grew serious. "You really do like her, don't you?"

"Yeah, I do."

"Well, go after her. Don't give up. Make her change her mind."

"Like you went after Jon?" He felt guilty as soon as his sarcastic comment was out of his mouth, yet he managed to release a faint chuckle when he expressed, "Tyla, you're so gullible at times."

"Yeah, like I did with Jon," Tyla proudly admitted. She didn't care who knew that she'd gone to Jon's apartment later that evening after he'd broken up with her and tried to persusde him to change his mind. "And I'm not gullible," she objected. "I just don't believe in giving up so easily on the people you love."

"I can't make her change her mind about not wanting to be in a relationship any more than I can change yours about wanting Jon back."

"Say what you want. I can't help how I feel."

"Well, I guess, neither can she."

Why can't I get him off my mind? Hope wondered as she tried to concentrate on the magazine she was perusing. *Because you've fallen for him, girl,* her inner voice answered back. *Hook, line and sinker.*

Never in a million years would she have thought that she'd fall for a younger man. But the age difference wasn't the problem. Hope was so afraid of being hurt again. Lance had been her knight in shining armor. As long as she had been with him, everything had been all right.

Leeza had been the kind of friend described in the Bible.

The kind depicted as loving all the time even in adversity. Two of the people she had loved and trusted the most in the world had betrayed her. How could she ever trust anyone again that implicitly? Tristen was so loving and caring, every woman's dream come true. But then, Lance had been, also. She couldn't refrain from making the comparison.

Until now, Hope had been able to repudiate all the advances men had thrown at her. She'd succeeded at first, too, with Tristen, but it wasn't long before he'd discovered the key to her heart. She found herself wondering what he was doing at this very moment. She even formed a mental picture of him with his fine physique horseback riding or just walking into a room. The mere thought took her breath away.

Chapter 27

As soon as all the daytime E.R. registration clerks had arrived at the hospital Monday morning, they were called to an emergency staff meeting. The supervisor informed them that numerous amounts of data errors had been discovered in their computer files and management would be meeting with each clerk within the next few days.

The upcoming layoffs, in addition to this latest news, really had everyone nervous.

As they made their way back to their stations after the meeting, Hope told Tyla, "I don't understand what's going on. We've never had this problem before. I mean, every now and then, somebody makes a mistake but nothing of this magnitude. I'm always extremely cautious when entering my information."

Tyla casually suggested, "Well, try not to worry about it.

They said they'll be meeting with us individually regarding our files. It's probably nothing to worry about."

"If it was nothing to worry about, we wouldn't have been called to the meeting."

Tyla didn't respond.

"Something's going on," Hope commented.

"What d'you mean?"

Hope lowered her voice. "I believe somebody at this hospital is trying to sabotage our work."

Tyla's eyes widened. "How can you say something like that?"

"Oh, Tyla, wake up and smell the coffee. People do that kind of stuff all the time. Don't you ever watch the news? You can't trust people. You are so naive."

"I don't understand you. You act like just because everybody's not contradictory like you that they don't have any sense."

Hope hissed, "Well, maybe when you've experienced life a little more, you'll see what I mean and grow up."

Tyla shouted, "You're not the only one who's had something bad happen to you! You're such a whiner! Why don't *you* grow up?" She marched back to her cubicle.

Instead of being upset with Tyla for going off on her, Hope felt a sense of satisfaction that her new young friend possessed a gumption to fend for herself when necessary.

Hope made her way toward Tyla's workstation. "I'm sorry," she uttered. "I didn't mean to upset you. You wanna grab some lunch in the cafeteria?"

Tyla kept her back to Hope. "If you want to."

"Okay."

Hope smiled as she walked away.

By Friday, the tension in the hospital E.R. was so thick you could cut it with a chain saw. Before Hope had come in, LaPorsha had run into Tyla, telling her that word was spreading that Hope had somehow gotten into the other registration clerks' computers and was sabotaging the data that they had inputted into the system. And since Hope's files were apparently the only ones that had not been tampered with, it was quite obvious that she was the culprit.

Tyla didn't like gossip and especially not about someone she cared about. She quickly dismissed the rumor until she was called into their supervisor's office later that day and questioned extensively about some of the data in her own files. When Tyla got back to her desk, her mind was full of questions about Hope's innocence. Yet, she didn't want to accuse Hope if she wasn't guilty.

During the next three weeks after all the clerks except for Hope had been continually reprimanded regarding incorrect data in their files, Tyla could not keep quiet any longer. The Friday before Christmas, while they were eating lunch in the hospital cafeteria, Tyla decided to confront Hope. Tyla was nervous. What if she was wrong?

She studied Hope's face so she could observe her reaction when she responded. "Hope, I need to ask you something and the only way I know to do it is to just come out and ask."

Chewing on her salad, Hope looked at Tyla and said, "Okay. Ask me. What is it?"

"Word around the E.R. is that everybody's computer files have been tampered with except yours. People are saying that somebody's changing our data."

Hope's eyes grew huge. "I told you somebody's been sabotaging our work. Does anybody know who it is?"

Tyla eyed her newfound friend. "Rumor has it that it's you."

Hope nearly choked on her salad. "What? You think— I can't believe you think I'd do something like that." Her fork made a clinking noise as it fell onto her plate. "Is that how little you think of me, Tyla? I thought you and I had become friends."

Regret rose in Tyla's belly. "We are friends. I ju-ju—"

Hope shook her head. "No, we're not friends. Not if you'd think that about me."

Tyla wiped her mouth with her paper napkin. "Well, Hope, the rest of us have gotten reprimanded several times for incorrect data in our files. You're the only registration clerk who hasn't. And when word first started to spread about the layoffs, you kept talking about how you can't afford to lose your job."

"That doesn't mean I did it. Tyla, think about it. I also told you somebody was sabotaging the files. Would I have said that if *I* was doing it? And if I was, wouldn't I change some of my own data, too, in order for people not to suspect me?"

Tyla mentally agreed that it couldn't be Hope. Perhaps

someone was trying to make Hope look guilty. Tyla didn't know what to believe.

Hope observed the confused expression on Tyla's face. "You don't believe me."

Tyla admitted, "I don't know what to believe."

Hope stood. "Well, you know what? I don't care what you believe. If this is how you treat your friends, then I'd rather us go back to being enemies. At least then, I knew where I stood with you." She grabbed her tray and walked away.

Tyla called out to her, but Hope didn't stop or look back.

Chapter 28

Three days later, Christmas Day, Hope still wasn't speaking to Tyla and continued to ignore all her phone calls. Since the children had spent Thanksgiving with their father, they were having Christmas with Hope. Tristen was coming by later to take Brandon ice-skating.

Hope was more exhausted than ever before. She'd been putting in lots of overtime hours at the Junction so that the kids could have a decent Christmas, in addition to life's basic necessities. During each monthly checkup with her doctor, he warned her that she needed to give up her part-time job and concentrate more on her health before she had another heart attack or a stroke.

She was fine. If she wasn't, why was she still able to keep going? As long as her body let her, she would continue pushing herself as she had been. Mercy had given her tomorrow off, but she had decided to put in as many hours as she could at the Junction.

When Tristen arrived at three-thirty to get Brandon, he commented on how tired Hope looked. He had finally accepted the fact that there was no future for the two of them. Nevertheless, every now and then, he would comment that she should marry him and let him take care of her. He was aware of how hard she worked to provide for her family and he was worried about her. When he saw how exhausted she looked, he suggested that Ashlee and Brittney accompany him and Brandon so that their mother could get some rest while they were gone. Hope happily agreed.

Hope's last thoughts before dozing off on the sofa were of Tristen and how he seemed to really care for her and how nice it was to have someone look after her for a change.

Hope had not a clue how long she'd been asleep until she stared groggily at the clock on the living room wall and saw that it was after six o'clock. She attempted to get up, but it felt as though all her energy had been drained from her body. She tried a few more times to lift herself from the sofa but couldn't move. She felt paralyzed. Panic struck at her very core.

She'd never felt like this before although she had noticed lately that she didn't seem to have as much energy as she normally did, but once she forced herself to get going, she was usually okay. She decided to just remain on the sofa and try again later. By seven o'clock, she was still in the same spot when the children and Tristen returned.

When Tristen saw the look of lethargy about her, he was

immediately at Hope's side. He knelt beside her and took her hand.

"Hope, are you okay? What's wrong?"

She sluggishly answered, "I do-don't kno-know. I ca-can't ge-get up."

"Come on," Tristen said as he scooped her up into his arms. "I'm taking you to the emergency room." To the three teenagers, he said, "Come on, guys."

Tristen gently set her onto the front seat of his SUV and buckled her seat belt while the teenagers climbed into the back. He didn't know how many red lights he ran on the way to the hospital. He carried her inside and placed her carefully on a waiting room chair and instructed Brandon to sign her in.

After the staff had gotten her registered, a nurse appeared with the requested wheelchair. Since only two people were allowed to go back with her, Tristen offered to stay in the waiting area with Brittney so Brandon and Ashlee could accompany her. However, Hope reached for his hand. When he held his hand out to her, she grabbed it.

"Yo-you com' wit m-me?"

Oh, God, is it a stroke this time?

Tristen knew if it was that time was of the essence, but he couldn't just jump ahead of her children if they weren't all right with it.

He looked at Brandon. "Is that okay with you, Brandon?"

Brandon nodded. "Sure. Me and Ash'll stay here." Looking at his sister, he asked, "That okay with you, Ash?"

Ashlee's eyes were consumed with a dreadful fear. "That's okay, but let us know what's wrong as soon as you find out."

Tristen grinned and said, "Will do." Grabbing Brittney with his free hand, he said, "Come on, Brit."

As the nurse wheeled Hope away, Hope and Tristen were still holding hands.

Tyla was frantic when she got off the phone. She turned to her mother.

"That was Tristen. He's with Hope and the kids at Mercy. He just took Hope to the E.R."

Myah's eyes grew huge. She walked toward her daughter. "What's wrong?"

"He doesn't know. The doctor hasn't seen her yet. I told him we'd be there in a few minutes."

The two women threw on their coats and grabbed their pocketbooks.

As they made their way out the front door, Tyla said, "I'll drive my car."

Myah followed and jumped in on the passenger side. When they got to the hospital, they met up with Brandon and Ashlee in the waiting area and sat with them until they saw Tristen walking toward them.

All four of them jumped up at the same time.

Tristen breathed a sigh of relief. "Her blood's low. That's why she was so weak. She's just run herself down. They're going to put her on some iron and keep her overnight."

Brandon and Ashlee threw their arms around Tristen.

Ashlee looked up at Tristen. "Can we see her?"

"Sure," Tristen answered. "They're moving her to her room now. Number three fifty-two." Removing his cell phone from its pouch, he said, "Here, Brandon, call your dad and let him know about your mom."

Brandon took the phone and placed the call. When he was through, he handed it back to Tristen. "He said he'll be here in twenty minutes."

They made their way to the elevator. As soon as Hope saw them enter her room, her heart swelled with elation. Tyla, Myah and Tristen stood back so Ashlee and Brandon could give her a hug. Then it was Tyla's turn. Next was Myah's. After a few minutes, everybody except Tristen had left the room.

Tristen pulled up a chair close to the bed, sat down and took Hope's hand in his.

Hope smiled through tears. "Thank you, Tristen. I don't know what I would've done without you or what the kids would've done if they'd found me like that by themselves." Her speech had improved although she was talking a little slower than usual.

Tristen grinned. "Your kids are smart. I think they would've handled themselves pretty well. They would've called 911 or driven you here themselves."

Hope closed her eyes momentarily. "Whew. I had no idea what hit me like that all of a sudden."

"Are you going to stop being hardheaded and listen to your doctor now?"

"You bet. Sooner or later, I'm bound to run out of second chances." She attempted a smile.

Tristen's tone grew serious. "Marry me, Hope, and let me take care of you and the kids. I love you so much. I want to be with you for the rest of my life."

"You're so sweet, Tristen. One of a kind. You know I can't marry you, but if I ever change my mind, you'll be the first to know. That is, of course, if you haven't been snatched up by some woman by then."

Tristen looked deep into her eyes. "You're the one I want. You're the only one for me. But I understand you're still hurting. Let me know if you change your mind."

Hope grinned awkwardly. "I will."

Suddenly it dawned on her that perhaps she'd left the door open for her and Tristen since she'd said *if* she changed her mind.

It was a new year and Hope had made a New Year's resolution to take better care of herself. That included not only her physical well-being but also her spiritual one. As soon as she'd gotten out of the hospital twelve days ago, she'd called her supervisor at the Junction and given him a verbal resignation effective immediately. She didn't know how she and the children were going to fare materially, but for the first time in a long while, money was no longer a major priority in her life. Her full-time job at Mercy would just have to do. That was, if she still had a job after the layoffs.

A few people had already gotten their pink slips during the month of December, including Tyla, since she was one of the last ones hired. Hope felt bad for them, especially so close to Christmas. But it hadn't taken Tyla long to land another part-time job. Since Hope had quit her job at the Junction, thereby opening up a vacancy, she had immediately put in a few good words about Tyla to the store's manager.

Six days ago, the hospital administrators had held a meeting with the registration clerks informing them that they had performed an internal investigation regarding the erroneous computer files. It had been discovered that another clerk had been observing other clerks as they logged on to their computers. The clerk was able to recall the passwords and logged into the hospital's file system at his or her own desk and entered incorrect data under coworkers' and even his or her own name but not Hope's, in order to make it appear as though Hope were the one doing it.

Although the administrators would not divulge the individual's name, rumor around the E.R. was that it was sixty-year-old Tabitha Peavy, who feared that she would be forced to take an early retirement due to the layoffs. Tyla had apologized profusely to Hope for suspecting her. Hope had assured her that she could see how she appeared to be guilty and that in anybody else's shoes, she probably would have thought the same thing.

Today was Hope's first time back in church since the break-up of her marriage three years ago. The Jeffersons had been so encouraging to her and her children. She now felt that she had gained not only another daughter in Tyla but also a dear friend. As Hope looked around after the service at her three-some, she was happy that they seemed to be making new friends already. The congregation was very warm and inviting.

Afterward, back at Myah's, Hope chuckled when she asked Tyla, "Do you remember that Scripture you threw upside my head the day we were at the hospital talking about the layoffs?"

Tyla grinned broadly. "Matthew, chapter six, verses twenty-five through thirty-four. What about 'em?"

Hope looked at Tyla. "I read those verses every night before I go to bed now. I need to have them embedded in my brain so I can keep going and not give up. My children and I have been through a lot these last few years, but we're still standing. I guess God was watching over us and taking care of us even when I didn't realize it. Otherwise, how could we have made it through?"

Tyla smiled. "Well, God knows our needs better than we do. He didn't promise us life would be easy, but he did promise that he would help us along the way."

Hope said, "Yes, he did, and I'm so thankful for that."

Myah released a happy sigh of relief at the heartfelt words of wisdom her daughter had just expressed.

Chapter 29

Hope had made it through another week in the E.R. She had to admit that although she missed the extra income from working part-time at the Junction, it felt really good to be able to come home after a hard day's work and just relax in the tub.

With the children at their father's, she found this was the perfect time for her to light some candles in the bathroom and try one of the at-home spa treatments she'd purchased recently. Since she couldn't afford the more expensive ones at the spa, she'd opted for the little packets of scented sea salt she could just add to her bathwater.

As she relaxed in her aromatic bathwater under the soft glow of the candles, she meditated on the scriptural text she'd read with the children that morning before they'd dashed off to school and to work.

The scripture was Psalm 26:2. *Examine me. Prove me. Try*

me. She thought about the ways in which she'd been examined, proven and tried.

All the time Hope had felt abandoned by God, he was still watching over her and her family and guiding them back to him. She now welcomed and asked God to examine her—to test her—because in doing so, it gave her the opportunity to demonstrate the depth of her loyalty to him.

The anger she held in the past had consumed her soul, her entire spirit. Stressing her heart and heaping more burdens on her than she could carry. Humbly, she had begun to seek God in prayer, begging him for the strength to move on, something she chastised herself for not doing from the beginning. Initially, it had not been easy trying to talk to a God who seemed so remote and negligent, while she struggled with her petitions. But it became easier over time.

Gradually, she felt her weighed-down heart become lighter. She couldn't recall exactly when it began to happen, but daily supplication lead to reading a Bible text each day, both of which started off as difficult chores before becoming a welcomed personal routine.

Tristen was always doting over Hope, expressing genuine concern for her well-being. Who could resist a man like him? Yet, she still didn't trust her heart when it came to men. Maybe she didn't really trust herself, either, fearing she would ruin the friendship and admiration of someone as special as him. If only she could love him the way he wanted and deserved to be loved. Her emotions remained raw. Perhaps one day romance would be on her agenda, but for now, Hope felt happy and content with her life.

* * *

Five months later, the day of Brandon's high school graduation had finally come. As his name was called, he strolled proudly across the football field to receive his diploma. All of his family, plus his new family, the Jeffersons and their mates, stood up in the bleachers, applauding loudly, waving and yelling his name. He happily waved back.

Afterward, they took him out to eat at his favorite restaurant. The Jeffersons were throwing an outdoor party for him tomorrow at Myah's.

The next day, the party was under way with much dancing, eating and socializing. When "The Hustle," one of Tyla's favorite old tunes, began playing, she grabbed Brandon and Hope by their hands and started doing the dance. Tristen got hold of Ashlee and Brittney and all three joined in. Everybody else present followed suit, having a ball.

After the party was over, Tyla was helping clean up when her mother entered the kitchen and told her that she had a visitor in the living room. Tyla ceased wiping the kitchen table and asked, "Who is it, Momma?"

She wondered if her mother was all right. She had a somewhat troubled look on her face. "It's Jon." Myah's tone was a soft whisper.

Immediately, Tyla saw Tristen's back straighten. His jaw clinched like granite, he took off toward the direction of the living room.

Tyla quickly caught up with him. Putting one hand on his back and grabbing his arm with her other hand, she begged, "Tristen, please. Let me handle this."

It took every fiber of his being for Tristen to will himself to back away.

Tyla longed to see Jon again, but she wasn't sure if her heart could take it. As she made her way to the living room, she wrestled with the host of emotions playing tic-tac-toe with her heart.

Jon was sitting on the love seat, the spot where he and Tyla used to lounge whenever he came by. He stood and took a couple of steps toward her. She immediately noticed that he looked a little thin. Her emotions pulled one end of her heart to the other. She wanted to run into his arms in spite of her good sense.

"Hi," she managed to say.

"Hi," he echoed. "I wanted to call first and see if you'd meet me somewhere, but I couldn't get up the nerve. I drove through your neighborhood four times before I got up the courage to stop and take a chance on you talking to me. I can understand if you don't want to."

Tyla's tone was soft and gentle as she stepped closer to him. "Of course I want to talk to you. Do you want to sit in here or out on the porch?"

"The porch would be nice." He couldn't face any more of her family. At least not now. He'd been relieved when he'd seen Tyla's mother outside when he'd finally pulled into the driveway. Even though he'd hurt her daughter, Myah still treated him kindly.

He opened the door and followed Tyla out onto the wooden swing.

Tyla asked, "How've you been?"

Tyla and her mother were the only people he knew whom you could hurt and they'd still be concerned about how *you* were doing.

"Miserable, but getting better. What about you?"

"Surviving."

Jon remarked warmly, "You're a special person, Tyla. You have such a good heart. You don't deserve what I did to you and I'll never forgive myself."

"Is that why you moved away?"

"Yes."

She nodded in thought. "You did hurt me. I can't tell you the number of times I tried to stop loving you. If I could have, I think it would've helped me not to hurt so much. Even though you broke up with me and called off the wedding, deep down inside, I wanted to believe it was because you loved me."

Jon felt a sense of relief. He still loved her more than she really knew, or maybe she did know.

Tyla expressed, "The night you told me what you did, I could tell how much it was tearing you up inside. The pain on your face and in your voice told me. And the way you cried. I'd never seen you cry like that until then. Even though I was hurt and angry, my heart broke for you."

Jon looked into her eyes. "I'll regret what I did for the rest of my life. I lost a good friend in you and my future wife. My relationship with you and your family will never be the same because of what I did."

Tyla said, "You didn't lose me as a friend. And as far as my family, all we can do is take one day at a time. There's always hope. Never give it up."

Jon nodded.

As they sat quietly and gazed up at the stars, she giggled and said, "Do you remember the time when you, me, Tristen, Torey and Terrell took off one weekend and went to Atlanta to the Fernbank Science Center there? We were in the planetarium looking up at the stars and all of a sudden, we heard snoring."

Jon let out a light chuckle. "Yeah, Tristen was knocked out, snoring up a storm."

"Yeah," Tyla said, "but what was even funnier was when he woke up and we were all gone, and he didn't remember where he was."

Jon added, "He said he was sleeping so good he thought he was home in his bed."

Their laughter was music to each other's ears. A brief silence fell between them.

Tyla asked, "So do you like living in Birmingham?"

"Yeah, it's nice. You know me—I'm a Southern boy."

"Did you find a job there in the medical engineering field?"

Jon nodded. "Yeah. At the university medical center there."

"That's good. You like your job?"

"Yeah. It's cool." Jon shot her a curious look. "How are things with you? How's school? Things still working out at the hospital?"

"School's going good. They're having a major layoff at Mercy. Since I was one of the last ones hired, I got my pink slip six months ago."

"I'm sorry."

"It's okay. I'm working part-time at the Junction."

"That's good. Still doing your modeling, too?"

"Yeah."

"Good."

Jon grasped Tyla's hand and their fingers intermingled. "I'm glad you're okay."

Tyla gave his hand a little squeeze. "I'm glad you are, too."

Tristen had been secretly standing near the living room window eavesdropping on Tyla and Jon's conversation. If she knew it, she'd pitch a fit. He didn't care. He was her big brother and had to make sure she was okay. He tried to move away from the window without disturbing the curtains or making any noise. Tyla was so resilient. As long as she was happy, that was all that mattered to him.

Jon looked down at his and Tyla's hands, each still holding the other. He didn't want to let go.

"Well," he said, "I guess I better be going. I've got to get up early in the morning for the drive back home."

Tyla felt her heart drop. "When will you be back?"

He released her hand and stood. "I don't know. Soon, I hope."

They walked side by side to Jon's car, not holding hands, but just enjoying the closeness of each other. When they reached the Lexus, they stopped and looked at one another one last time.

Jon said, "You take care of yourself."

"You, too."

Tyla stood back so he could open the door. They quietly

wrapped their arms around each other and stayed that way for several seconds. Then Jon planted a delicate kiss on her left cheek before climbing inside his car.

His window was down. He said goodbye one last time.

Tyla waved.

It seemed as though it only took him a split second to back out of the driveway and take off down the street, reminding Tyla of how time went by so slowly when you were young and at the speed of a bullet as you got older.

As she made her way back to the house, her spirit felt renewed. Upon walking through the front door, she yelled, "Tristen, com'ere with your bighead self. I know you were eavesdropping on my conversation with Jon."

Tyla recalled the concerned look in her brother's eyes when their mother had quietly announced Jon's arrival. It had reassured Tyla of how blessed she was to have him as her big brother, in spite of his being overbearing at times. She wouldn't want it any other way.

She found Tristen in the kitchen, attempting to appear innocent.

"What makes you think I was listening?" he asked with a wounded look on his face.

"Don't go there with me, Tristen. I told you I could handle the matter myself without your help."

His grunt only sparked a low chuckle from her as she shook her head at his response.

Tristen had lost a dear friend out of this, too, and it was only a matter of time for the healing to begin with renewed hope, bridging the gap between old friends.

Big brothers were fun to have around, but sometimes, they all could be one huge pain in the neck. And to think, God had blessed her with three of them.